MIDNIGHT MARAUDER

AND THE

PRESIDENT

OF THE UNITED STATES

Roy Clinton

ISBN: 9781790188055

Independently Published

Top Westerns Publishing (www.TopWesterns.com), 3730 Kirby Dr., Suite 1130, Houston, TX 77098. Contact info@TopWesterns.com for more information.

Cover and Book Design by Teresa Lauer: info@teresalauer.com.

ROY CLINTON

MIDNIGHT MARAUDER
AND THE
PRESIDENT
OF THE UNITED STATES

A Series of Western Novels
Featuring the Adventures of
John Crudder

Other Books by Roy Clinton

Lost
Midnight Marauder
Return of Midnight Marauder
Revenge of Midnight Marauder

These books and others can be found on
www.TopWesterns.com and *www.Amazon.com*.
Audio versions of the books can be found on
www.Audible.com as well as on iTunes.

Dedicated to my late grandfather,

Pappy.

From him I learned to love drinking coffee and getting up
early.

It is his name,

Clinton Roy,

that I borrowed as the pseudonym for my novels.

Table of Contents

PREFACE

1873, New York City

M r. President, it is an honor to meet you!" When Howard Hastings told me we would have an important visitor, I had no idea he was talking about President Grant. I stood awkwardly in Howard's living room at Howard's side as I spoke to the President.

"Mr. Crudder," the President coughed for several seconds and said, "Pardon me. It is I who is honored to meet you."

President Ulysses S. Grant was a commanding presence. I guess that is an understatement considering he was the commander of the Union forces in the war that divided our nation. Although he was a bit shy of average height, there was an air about him in two ways. First, he had the countenance of a man who was very sure of himself. Second, a dark cloud seemed to follow him as he moved due to his incessant cigar smoking. I recalled hearing that Grant smoked twenty cigars a day. He also enjoyed chewing them. He picked up both habits from his long years in the field commanding the troops in the War Between the States.

In a book written by General Horace Porter, Grant was quoted as saying,

I had been a light smoker previous to the attack on Donelson [Fort Donelson in Tennessee]. After that battle, I acquired a fondness for cigars by reason of pure accidental circumstance.... In the accounts published in the papers, I was represented as smoking a cigar in the midst of the conflict; and many persons, thinking, no doubt, that tobacco was my chief solace, sent me boxes of the choicest brands.... As many as ten thousand were soon received. I gave away all I could get rid of, but having such a quantity on hand I naturally smoked more than I would have done under ordinary circumstances, and I have continued the habit ever since.

In addition, General Sherman ingratiated himself to Grant by bringing him five thousand cigars from Havana during the War Between the States. Grant was one year into his second term and, from all accounts, a very fine president. What I have heard most about him is how he stabilized the economy that had been devastated by the war. It puzzled me as to why the President would want to meet me and why he would say he was honored to do so. I bowed slightly as I shook the President's hand.

"Mr. President," I said, as I tried to make sense of my thoughts, "I am at your disposal though I can't conceive of how I might be of service to you."

"Mr. Crudder. May I call you John?"

"Certainly, Mr. President."

"Well I need your help because," the President coughed again. "a few days ago, Jay Cooke & Company, the investment bank and brokerage house that has financed some of the railroads, totally collapsed."

"Mr. President, this is the first I have heard of that. Of course I know of the brokerage house since they have been instrumental in helping many railroads secure the funds necessary to expand."

"But to my knowledge," said the President, "I don't think Great National Railroad has ever issued bonds to be sold through that company. Is that correct?"

"Indeed it is, Mr. President. Great National has not done business with Jay Cooke & Company. However, in the past, we did issue bonds with some other brokerage houses when my father was alive. All of those bonds have been paid in full to the investors. Our railroad is debt free. We do have some temporary debt to suppliers but no long-term debt. Isn't that true, Mr. Hastings?"

Howard Hastings straightened his back, cleared his throat, and said in a voice almost an octave above his normal speaking voice, "That's right, John, Mr. Crudder. I mean, that's right, Mr.

President."

"As I was saying," President Grant continued, "Cooke & Company has become insolvent. They were not able to sell all of the bonds issued by Northern Pacific Railroad. The resulting panic has rippled through the railroad industry, has caused a run on the banks, and even closed the Stock Market, as you are undoubtedly aware."

I was dumbfounded at what I was hearing. I knew nothing of a panic that involved the railroads. But I also realized I had been traveling most of the past three weeks and arrived in New York City less than an hour before the President knocked on the door of Mr. Hastings' mansion.

"I'm sorry, Mr. President," said Howard Hastings. "Mr. Crudder arrived in New York from Texas only a few minutes ago. I was just getting ready to tell him of the financial troubles in the city when you arrived."

I was speechless. It sounded like, at the very least, there was an earthquake that was rocking the railroads that might spread to the entire country and beyond. Still I didn't know why President Grant would want to see me.

"Mr. Crudder. John," said the President, "I understand you have an extraordinary head for business and you have a reputation for knowing how to handle delicate situations."

"Thank you, Mr. President. But Mr. Hastings is the one with business acumen. I haven't had much to do with the business since I sold the company several years ago. My talents lie with herding cattle and building fence. I'm a rancher these days and an outsider when it comes to the goings on in New York."

"Come now, John," said the President. "You own one of the largest railroad companies in the country. I appreciate your modesty but you are a shrewd businessman. You have built on what was inherited from your father and the company is now stronger than ever."

"Mr. President, I sold Great National Railroad several years ago. Mr. Hastings has been running it ever since."

"It is true," said the President, "that you did sell the company. But isn't it more accurate that you sold part of the company?"

Mr. Hastings' mouth opened and he turned to me with a shocked expression. I could see he had many questions but I had hoped to have this discussion with him in private and at a more opportune time.

"What's he talking about, John?" asked Hastings. "You sold all of the company. I would have known if you hadn't."

I couldn't look Howard in the eye. As I stared at my boots, I searched for the right words to tell my old friend I had not been honest with him. I had led Mr. Hastings to believe I had completely divested myself of Great National and that he was running it all. What he didn't know is that I had retained a controlling interest in the railroad. The shadow corporation I set up operated silently and duplicated any decisions Howard made.

"Howard, I had hoped to be able to tell you this later today—but it's true, I haven't been entirely honest with you. I did sell the railroad, that is, I sold part of it. At the time I made the transaction, I did so because I wasn't cut out to be the businessman like my father. I didn't get the same joy from the day-to-day decisions of running a large company that you did. I sold about a third of the company so I could retain a controlling interest. The reason I did that was in case I might someday wish to return to the company in some capacity. I was afraid my decision to sell it in its entirety might have been an impulsive decision of youth that might prove to be unwise in the long run.

"Howard," I continued, "I hope you can forgive me for deceiving you as I have. I never meant to lie to you. As I told you when I sold part of the company, I wanted you to be the CEO of Great National for life. That has never changed. The only thing different is, no group of shareholders can push you out of the company. The only one who can fire you is me. And that will never happen."

"Well, I'm enjoying this little homecoming you're having," said the President. "But unfortunately, we don't have time for that. The country is in a crisis and, John, I need your help if it is going to survive."

"I'm at your disposal, Mr. President."

"I was hoping you would say that. And John, I need your help for another reason. Not only do I need your influence in the railroad industry but I also need your, shall I call them, problem solving skills. I need the help of the Midnight Marauder."

I was shocked at what I was hearing. How could my secret have come out? How could the President of the United States know of my alter ego that cleaned up the evil that was controlling my beloved Bandera, Texas? I tried to speak, but the words just wouldn't come. I turned to Hastings with a question on my face. He gently shook his head indicating he had not divulged my secret.

"Don't worry, John. Mr. Hastings has not breached your trust. All I'm saying is you may have some knowledge of the Midnight Marauder and may know how to contact him."

President Grant cocked his head slightly as he smiled and let his words settle in. It was obvious he believed my connection to the Midnight Marauder was more than just knowing how to contact him.

"Mr. President," I said as I looked for the right words, "I am at a loss to know how to respond. Please forgive me if I can't think of an appropriate answer."

"John, I'm not interested in bringing any trouble to you. And I want you to know, when I put the pieces together and realized you must be the contact for the Midnight Marauder, I didn't share my information with the governor of Texas or anyone else. I don't intend for anyone outside of this room to ever know of this connection.

"From all accounts I've heard, the Midnight Marauder did the state of Texas and Bandera, in particular, a favor by eliminating the evil men and women who were intent on destroying that town. What I want to know is if the Midnight Marauder would be able to do for our country what he did for Bandera?"

I hung my head as I continued looking for an appropriate response. After a long few moments, I raised my head and looked President Grant in the eye.

"Mr. President, I am at your disposal. And I will be glad to contact the Midnight Marauder on your behalf. I'm sure he will understand how he might be of service."

CHAPTER 1

Howard Hastings had been the CEO of Great National Railroad for several years, ever since I sold a significant part of it and moved out west. From all accounts, he was an excellent businessman. The company continued to grow under his leadership. I purposely kept myself at arm's length from the company allowing him to run it as he saw fit. What Mr. Hastings did not know is that I had created another corporation in secret that was in essence a holding company for the remaining company stock. Decisions made by Mr. Hastings were duplicated in the holding company so that he ran the entire railroad company. I never intended to get involved again in the day-to-day operations.

***

In the summer of 1873, Mr. Hastings was interrupted by an

urgent knock on his office door. When he opened it, he was surprised to see several men he had gotten to know in the course of business. William Summerall headed the group. Hastings knew Summerall had put together a group of investors that had already taken control of several smaller railroads and was intent on expanding their reach to as many others as possible. Mr. Hastings was now aware of Summerall's attempt to purchase controlling interest in Great National.

"Mr. Hastings. I am J. William Summerall. My associates and I would like to have a word with you."

"Bill, I know who you are. We've met on several occasions. I'm not sure why you're acting as if we don't know each other. Come on in and tell me your business."

As the group entered Hastings' office, Howard noticed that included in the delegation were two uniformed police officers. When all were in place, Summerall held up a piece of paper, addressed Hastings, and handed him the document.

"Mr. Hastings, this is Buckminster Carmichael," said Summerall as he pointed to the man next to him. "Together, Mr. Carmichael and I, along with these good people gathered here, have bought Great National Railroad. That is, we have bought enough so that it is now under our control. Your services as CEO are no longer required. I would like to ask you to vacate the premises now and not ever enter this office again. I'm sure you will find I am entirely within my rights. If you don't believe me, you can check with your attorney and you will find you no longer have control."

Summerall had been a member of the New York Stock Exchange for more than four decades. He was in his late sixties. Rotund and pompous, Summerall literally filled every room he entered. His voice was louder than any other and he seemed to always be just a few words away from a deep belly laugh. In nearly every gathering while shaking hands with those assembled, he would throw his head back every few sentences and let out a loud chortle, slap someone on the back, and move on to the next most influential person in the room.

Buckminster Carmichael was at least thirty years junior of Summerall and had obtained his seat on the exchange just a few years before. He was fit and trim, and was decidedly introverted. Just shy of six feet tall, he was a bit shorter than Summerall. He walked a step or two behind Summerall and would only shake hands or speak to those who spoke to him first. He had sandy blonde hair and could easily pass for someone ten years younger. Both men sported handlebar mustaches.

Summerall motioned the officers to move forward. "These gentlemen are here to make sure you take your personal possessions and leave this office immediately."

"This is most irregular," said Hastings. "You can't throw me out of my own office. I'll get my attorney to come here and he will straighten it all out."

"You are free to contact anyone you would like after you leave," said Summerall. "But for now, you have ten minutes to collect what is yours and leave. And you're not to touch any of the company files. You may only take those things that belong to you. These policemen will verify you don't have any company property in your possession and then escort you from the building."

Howard Hastings couldn't believe what he was hearing. How could these men throw him out of his office? Why was this happening? How could they have possibly taken control of Great National Railroad?

Hastings gathered a few possessions from his desk and walked slowly toward the door. One of the policemen took him by the elbow and tried to hurry Hastings along. Howard jerked his arm free and said, "I know the way out of the office and I can leave without any of your help!"

The policeman backed away and allowed Hastings to walk unimpeded the rest of the way. As he entered the outer office, there was shock on the faces of secretaries and other office workers as they watched him leave. Outside, Hastings couldn't believe what had happened to him. He stood on Wall Street and looked back at the office where he had worked for the past thirty years.

Howard walked toward his home on Fifth Avenue. As he walked, he became aware of a great deal of commotion around him. There was panic on the street but he couldn't discern the source.

"THE STOCK EXCHANGE IS CLOSED! THE EXCHANGE IS CLOSED!" shouted several well-dressed men whose suits were wet with sweat. As Hastings watched, he saw scores of people coming out of the stock exchange shouting the same thing. Howard stopped one of the passing men and asked what was going on.

"They say the railroads are collapsing," said the man. "President Grant has closed the New York Stock Exchange. That has never happened before! I'm going to my bank and get my money out. You better do the same. It won't be long before the banks close, too."

Hastings turned from the subway station and hurried to the telegraph office to tell me what was happening. He thought together we could figure out what was going on.

Roy Clinton

CHAPTER 2

What does it mean to go home? Certainly part of it is going back to where you grew up. It's funny when I look back at my life, I feel like Bandera is my home. I've lived here for the past three years and have no desire ever to live anywhere else.

Part of going home is returning to that first time you felt you had a calling—a direction in life. For me, that was when I realized I wanted to study law. It was less about being a lawyer than it was about making sure everyone had an opportunity for justice. I realized that when I first learned about the Scales of Justice. It was then I realized most of the people in the world didn't have the advantages I had been afforded. Even Alvelda—who had been my nanny, playmate, and best friend, and whom I loved with all my heart—didn't have the chance to speak her mind and to do anything she wanted in life. She has had a great life—no doubt about that—but it was not by choice. Suppose, for example, she wanted to live somewhere else and do the same work she did for my father and mother. That was not her choice. Or suppose she wanted to open a café and cook the many wonderful meals she made for me but do it for other people. That was not her choice.

There were so many other examples in life of nice people, kind people, great people, who could have done so much more in their lives but they didn't have the choice. When I first came west, I met a man who had a dream of starting a cattle ranch. At the time, I didn't have any idea what that required. Now, I know he didn't have the capital required and never would have, simply because of his station in life. He didn't have a wealthy father and unlimited resources like I did.

I thought of the woman I had rescued from being raped behind the saloon in Fort Worth several months ago. I never knew her story—only that she worked in the saloon and had to put up with the pawing and inappropriate advances of men who were drunk and wanted to prove their manliness. Suppose her dream was to open a saloon of her own? That may or may not have been her goal in life. But suppose it was. Was there even the remotest chance she could accomplish that? Of course not. She didn't have the means.

About then it dawned on me there was more to my idea of balancing the Scales of Justice than seeing lawbreakers meet with justice. The economic injustice I saw all around me was in many ways harder for me to reconcile.

I determined then to have a talk with Charlotte and see what she thought about us trying to give away the fortune that had come our way. Actually, that was not even a question. Unless I completely misjudged Charlotte, she would be completely in line with my thoughts. She has never been focused on what money could buy. She was born to privilege as well. Not nearly on the same scale as I, but she was nonetheless the daughter of a man who owned the largest ranch in that part of Texas. Yet for her, she would have been just as happy on a small spread of only a few acres, a dozen head of cattle, and enough chickens to provide eggs for the family.

At this point, I knew my mission was two pronged. I would have to once again adopt the ruthless persona of the Midnight Marauder to right the abuse of people being treated unjustly. I also realized I needed to be looking for others who were hurting, or in need, or who just needed some help to make it through the next day. I knew I was one of the wealthiest people in the country but I didn't need any of the wealth. I had all I needed in my wife and my children and there wasn't anything else I desired or craved. Indeed, I counted myself as one of the most fortunate people in the world.

My mission was changing. I needed to use what I'd received to make a difference in other people's lives. The Good Book says, "To whom much is given, much is required." I have indeed been given much. I planned on making it my life's work to give what I could to others who need it. If Charlotte would share my vision, she will also be on a continual lookout to find people who need what we can so easily supply.

This may sound like a dichotomy, but the role of the Midnight

Marauder and the philanthropist I want to be are two sides of the same coin. In both roles, my mission—my job—is to see that the Scales of Justice always balance as far as I am able to do so.

***

Life for me started in New York City. I was raised with the best of everything, but I wasn't spoiled. My parents didn't dote on me. They instilled in me the need to work hard and study hard. My education includes two degrees from Harvard University—one of them in law—and a master's degree from Oxford.

It was my father's dream for me to join him in running Great National Railroad that he built from nothing. The good Lord knows I tried. I gave my best effort to becoming a businessman he would be proud of—and I was good at it—but being in business was never something I wanted or felt fulfilled doing.

Now I'm in a new life with a wife and two precious daughters. I was living the life of a gentleman rancher and felt life was perfect. Then one day, I received a telegram that I needed to go home to New York immediately.

John Crudder
H&F Ranch
Bandera, Texas

Please come quickly. I've just been fired from Great National.
Company may be sold or split up. Come soon as possible.

Howard Hastings
Fifth Avenue
New York City, New York

My father's company was at risk and I felt I was the only one who could save it. For justice to be served, the Midnight Marauder was needed in New York.

Although I looked forward to going back to my childhood home, I was going to have to admit to Howard Hastings I had not been totally transparent with him. I have an immense secret I have kept from him. My hope is it won't change how he thinks of me.

"John, I know you need to go," said Charlotte. "You take care of things in New York. We'll be fine while you're gone."

"I don't see how I can go, Charlotte," I said. "It's not right for me to leave you alone to take care of the girls by yourself."

"But she won't be alone," Slim said. "I did a good job raisin' Charlotte and I'll do a good job as grandpa. You do what you need to do. We'll be here when you get back."

I looked at both and nodded my thanks. It didn't take me but a few minutes to get packed and get Midnight saddled. I swung up and rode over to the porch.

"I'll ride Midnight to San Anton and take the stage to Kansas and then take the train to New York. I don't know how long I'll be gone, but I will be back as soon as possible. I'll do my best to be back by Christmas."

Charlotte came over so I leaned down and kissed her.

"Be careful," she shouted as I rode off.

I rode Midnight hard to San Antonio. At the livery stable, I made arrangements for them to care for him and paid for four months' board. It would take me about two and a half weeks to get to New York—that is, if all of my connections worked out.

At the stage office, I purchased passage all the way to Kansas City. I needed to make a quick stop in Fort Worth and felt that would delay me for about a day. Other than that, it looked like all of the stage connections would work out with a minimum amount of layover.

It was mid-September in the year of 1873. Charlotte and I have been married about two years and our lives together couldn't be any better. We have both healed from the injuries we sustained when Charlotte was kidnapped. I still shudder when I think of how close I came to losing her. The entire town council in Bandera turned out to be wicked and dishonest. In my role as Midnight Marauder, I had eliminated each of them along with a number of coconspirators.

I guess it was too much to hope the Midnight Marauder could permanently retire and I could just be a husband, a father, and a rancher. Claire and Cora look just like their mother. Watching them grow over the past year has been one of the greatest joys of my life.

CHAPTER 3

Boarding the stage in San Antonio, I was pleased to find there were only two other passengers. Two sisters, both schoolteachers, were headed to Kansas City to care for their ailing mother so we would be keeping company for the next two weeks.

In Texas, there really aren't four seasons. Summer lasts until September and then winter begins the next month. Autumn usually gets missed entirely. The leaves are green, then suddenly turn brown and fall. But this year, it seemed there was an abundance of color with leaves changing from yellow to red.

The temperature was already dropping and each of us was wearing a jacket. I knew before we got to Kansas City we were in for some really cold weather. The ladies sitting across from me seemed to be shivering already. Not to be critical, but I noticed the coats both ladies were wearing were threadbare. Initially, I wondered why they didn't bring something warmer for their journey. It finally occurred to me that living in that part of Texas, they didn't need much warmer clothes. Then, as an afterthought, I realized as schoolteachers, they likely didn't have a surplus of money to purchase something warmer.

I worried about how they were going to make it all the way to their destination without freezing. Since they boarded the stage before me, they had the two seats that faced forward. Just a few miles out of San Antonio, I realized while they had the view they wanted, they also had the wind coming in the open windows.

"I didn't properly introduce myself. My name is John Crudder," I said as I tipped my hat.

"My name's Sarah and this is my sister Hannah."

"I'm pleased to meet you ladies. The station agent told me the three of us will be sharing a stage all the way to Kansas City."

"That's right," said Hannah. "Our mother is ill and we need to go take care of her."

"In fact," said Sarah, "we don't know if we will even get there in time to see her again."

Both ladies had tears come to their eyes as they contemplated life without their mother. I wanted to say something to comfort them but realized I was well out of my depth. Even with Charlotte, I struggled to know how to respond to women when they were sad. My inclination was to fix it. I wanted to say something that would take away the hurt or offer some words of wisdom that would cheer them up.

Being married to Charlotte for the last two years had taught me that sometimes I sound the smartest when I just shut up. There were some things in life I couldn't fix. That was a hard lesson to learn, and to be truthful, I still hadn't completely learned it. But at least on that day, I said nothing more for a while and just stared out the window.

The weather turned progressively colder over the next couple of hours. The sisters were obviously cold. While I wanted to respect their need for silence, I also felt I needed to address their need for warmth.

"Ladies, if I could be so bold, I know you selected the seats you wanted for our trip. And I can appreciate the fact that from where you sit, you get the clearest view of the journey. But I also realize you're getting the wind directly in your faces. In my seat, I don't get as much scenery, but it is much warmer since there is no wind at all. If you would rather sit here, I would be glad for you to have this seat."

"Thank you, sir," said Hannah.

"Yes, thank you," added Sarah.

They wasted no time in moving to the other side of the coach. I watched as they got up simultaneously and moved on either side of me before I could even get up.

"This is much better," said Hannah.

"It is. Thank you," said Sarah.

I was detecting a pattern here. Hannah always spoke first and it was as though Sarah always completed her thought.

"I have a question but I fear asking it for I might offend one or both of you. To me you appear to be about the same age. Are you twins?"

"Yes, we are," giggled Hannah.

"And we have been for all of our lives," laughed Sarah. "Sorry, that's just a bit of twin humor."

I had a huge grin on my face as I reached into my pocket and retrieved two tintypes.

"This is my wife Charlotte and our twin daughters, Claire and Cora."

"They're beautiful," said Hannah.

"Absolutely beautiful," added Sarah. "We don't meet many twins and we've never gotten to speak with the parents of twins, other than our own parents."

"You're the first twins, other than my own, I've ever met," I said. "Charlotte and I have wondered what life will be like for our girls. Before they started talking, they would make sounds to each other and it was almost like they had their own language. They would look at each other and speak some gibberish and then laugh."

The ladies looked at each other and laughed.

"Twin language," they both said together and then laughed.

"We did that a lot when we were younger," said Hannah.

"And we still know what the other is thinking and can complete each other's sentences," said Sarah as they both laughed harder.

I joined in their laughing. It was like a dam burst for suddenly I didn't have any trouble knowing what to say to a woman. For the next several hours we talked about what it was like to be twins and I listened to stories of their adventures.

"One of our favorite things was to swap places in school so

our classmates and our teacher didn't know which twin we were," said Hannah.

"So some of the time," added Sarah, "people stopped trying to figure out which we were and would just call us 'Twin.'"

"Momma would always dress us alike," said Hannah.

"And we liked it until we became teenagers," said Sarah.

"Then we rebelled a bit and started to show our individuality," said Hannah.

"Not that you would really call us rebels," said Sarah.

"We just started to refuse to dress like the other," said Hannah.

"But once we got to be adults. . .," started Sarah.

"We decided it was great fun sometimes to dress alike and watch people stare at us thinking they were seeing double," said Hannah.

The sisters didn't know it but they had given me a great gift. It was as though I was sitting across from Claire and Cora as grown women telling me about life as a twin. I hung on to every story and laughed as hard as they did.

It took three more days to make it to Fort Worth. While we were enjoying our conversations, the temperature dropped and I knew the twins were very cold. Arriving in Fort Worth, I told the ladies I had some business to attend to and I would have to delay my journey by a day.

"Actually, John, we have been so cold…," said Hannah.

"That we were planning on spending the night here hoping it would be a bit warmer tomorrow," said Sarah, completing her sister's thought.

We all went over to the boarding house. The sisters rented a room and I went up to the room that I had kept for the past several years to pack several of my suits, shirts, and a topcoat into a large trunk. Back downstairs I made arrangements for the trunk to be delivered to the stage office. In New York, I would need the nice wardrobe I had acquired when I first arrived in Fort Worth.

When it became apparent my knowledge of the illegal activities of the Bandera town council placed those I love in jeopardy, I became the Midnight Marauder. And in an effort to have a place to stay out of the spotlight, I came to Fort Worth and adopted the alias of Robert Hamilton, English gentleman and clerk at a fine men's store. It was time for me to visit my old friend Mr. Asbury, who was now not only a purveyor of men's clothes, but also the owner of a large emporium that specialized with fine ladies' wear.

I walked down to the haberdashery and saw Mr. Asbury waiting on a customer. As I waited, and looked through several racks of clothes, I kept my hat on and my head down so Asbury couldn't see my face.

"I'm sorry to keep you waiting, sir," said Asbury. "How may I help you?"

"Well, mister, it's like this," I said in my strongest Texas twang. "I heared you had some clothes that could might near make a man into an English gentleman."

"Well, we do have some very fine clothes."

Just then, I looked up and tipped my hat back.

"Robert! What on earth are you doing here? I haven't heard a thing from you in over two years."

"Hello, Mr. Asbury. Much has happened in the past two years. I'm sorry I haven't had a chance to come by and see you. How have you been doin'?"

"Robert, I can't get over the transformation. You remind me of that cowboy who came here looking for a job about three years ago. What happened to that very proper British gentleman?"

"Oh, he's still there. I can call on him when needed," I said as I once again adopted the British brogue I used when selling clothes. Then going back to my Texan accent, "So tell me how things have been goin' for you."

"I can't tell you how great things have been. Your idea of opening the emporium was pure genius. The sales have far outstripped my greatest projections. And the sales at this store have also continued to grow. And Robert, I owe it all to you. I will forever be in your debt. But best thing of all; I'm engaged! I asked Miss Dawson to be my wife, and she said yes. That never would have happened if you hadn't encouraged me to open the emporium and hire her as manager."

"I'm so glad to hear things have been goin' well for you. Mr. Asbury, there is somethin' I need from you."

"Just name it, Robert. I'll do anything for you I can."

"I appreciate that. Actually what I need is some help getting two ladies some clothes."

"I see," said Asbury with a look of mischief in his eye.

"It's not like that. You see, I'm on my way to Kansas City by stage and two sisters are on board. Their clothes are not nearly warm enough for the trip. What I would like to do is purchase them the clothes they need—several dresses each—along with the warmest coats you have. But I want to keep my involvement a secret."

"I can most certainly do that. Have them come by the emporium and I'll get them fixed up. I'll go over and tell Miss Dawson to take care of them and to charge it all to your account."

"That will be just fine. I'll stop over and pay the bill before I leave town. I have to go now. Oh, and Mr. Asbury, please have six of your finest wool blankets delivered to the stage office to accompany us tomorrow. I have a feelin' it's gonna get a lot colder before we make it to Kansas."

"I'll take care of all of that. Robert, it has been good to see you again. We need to have more time to catch up. Someday I want to hear all about your life. I have a feeling there is much about you I don't know."

"Maybe we'll have that chance, Mr. Asbury. So long for now."

I made my way over to the rooming house and knocked on the sisters' room.

"Hello, John," said Hannah. "We were just going to supper."

"Would you like to join us?" continued Sarah.

"I would indeed. Thank you for the invitation."

We walked down to the dining room and each of us ordered a

meal. After dessert and coffee, I got down to the subject at hand.

"The reason I knocked on your door is because I just had a visit with a friend of mine who lives here. I told him I was on my way to Kansas City and two sisters were traveling together. In our conversation, I told him you were going back home to care for your ailing mother. He said he hated to hear about your mother's illness but he especially hated for anyone to have to travel in such cold weather. Anyway, he said he wanted to do somethin' for you but that it had to be a secret. This man is very wealthy and he enjoys tryin' to make life better for others.

"He said he wants the two of you to go to Asbury Emporium and see the manager by the name of Miss Dawson. He said he has instructed her to get you each a new wardrobe and especially some nice heavy coats for your journey."

The sisters looked at each other, both with mouths hanging open. Then they started speaking.

"We don't know what to say," said Hannah.

"What a nice man," added Sarah.

They looked at each other again and began giggling.

"So which way," began Hannah.

"To the emporium?" said Sarah, once again completing the thought.

I paid the check and walked them out front of the rooming house. Pointing, I gave them directions and watched them skip down the boardwalk. It's hard to describe the feeling I had when I watched the sheer joy on the sister's faces. I watched as they disappeared around the corner and then I went inside and paid for the sisters' room for the evening. My instructions to the proprietor were very specific that I had to remain anonymous. In talking with the owner, I verified the bank was still making monthly payments on my behalf. Satisfied that all was in order, I retired to my room for the evening.

The next morning, I went to the stage office and smiled as I saw the sisters. They were wearing new dresses and wearing beautiful hats. Several extra pieces of luggage needed to be loaded. It looked to me like there would be a number of additional passengers. But as soon as the bags were loaded, the driver climbed up and called to his horses as he roused them from their rest.

"I thought there were more passengers joining us," I said as I looked across at the sisters.

They both laughed and told me that the additional bags were for them.

"We got several new dresses," said Hannah.

"And new coats," added Sarah as she also pointed to a large stack of blankets in the seat between them. "And they also sent along these blankets so we don't get cold. That certainly was nice of that man. I wish we knew who he was."

As we were passing the haberdashery, Mr. Asbury was in the doorway. I waved as we passed.

"Good to see you again, Robert. See you next time you're in town."

"Who is Robert?" asked Hannah.

"I thought your name is John," said Sarah.

"It is. He must've been speakin' to the driver."

"John, when we checked out of the boarding house . . .," began Hannah.

"They said our bill was already paid," continued Sarah. "Do you know anything about that?"

"I guess it was the same man who got you the new clothes," I said. Then I lowered my hat over my eyes and leaned back against the seat. "I don't mean to be bad company, ladies, but I think I'll take a little nap."

Roy Clinton

CHAPTER 4

In September 20 of 1873, about five days after John set out for New York City, the stock market suspended trading for the first time. For ten days, the markets were closed, hoping to curb the panic set up by the uncertainty in the nation's railroads. It seems that some of the once seemingly invincible railroads were struggling to survive.

Speculators and investors were betting heavily on railroad projects. For example, a second transcontinental railroad was undertaken by the Northern Pacific Railroad. A spirit of optimism permeated the country. The New York Stock Exchange would rank a railroad stock or corporate bond as to their estimated value, but no one knew for certain the value of the railroad's land holdings or the federal contracts they owned. There was an assumption that cash would continue to flow around the country and make it easy for people to purchase the goods they wanted.

Unscrupulous politicians and greedy railroad investors took

advantage of this atmosphere of optimism and were able to inflate the value of railroad stock. Jay Cooke & Company, one of the largest banks and investment firms in New York City, had several million dollars of railroad bonds that it was unable to market. It seems the gullibility of the nation ran headlong into the true value of the railroads. Concurrently, investors lost their enthusiasm for speculating further on anything having to do with the railroad industry.

Meanwhile the railroad companies in Europe began selling bonds for their own railroad expansion. Some investors in America began selling off their U.S. investments to purchase what looked to be more favorable bonds in Europe. Within a few weeks, there were more bonds available worldwide than there were investors who wanted to purchase them.

In September of 1873, Jay Cooke & Company filed for bankruptcy protection. That began a run on other banks across the country. It was thought if a bank the size of Cooke could fail, people needed to pull their money out of lesser banks while they still could. On the twentieth of that month, the New York Stock Exchange suspended trading and the market remained closed for ten days. Ultimately, more than one hundred banks would fail. This was the beginning of what would later be known as the Panic of 1873 and a worldwide depression that would last for six years.

Times were desperate around the country. Just three years earlier, President U.S. Grant successfully broke up an attempt by unscrupulous businessmen to corner the gold market. Corrupt politicians like Boss Tweed were giving all politicians a bad name. What the country didn't need was another scandal brought on by the railroads.

Quietly, President Grant contacted Howard Hastings of Great National Railroad. Hastings had always been known as a man of integrity and honor. President Grant had his assistant telegraph Hastings and arrange a secret meeting in New York City. Hastings agreed and invited his secret visitor to his Fifth Avenue mansion and instructed the staff to have the buggy bearing the visitor to unload at the rear entrance of the mansion. On the day of the meeting, Hastings hurried home to prepare for his visitor. Though he didn't know exactly who would be calling on him, he did know it was a person of influence and importance. The last person he expected was the President of the United States.

The buggy slowed as it approached the house. A butler stood at the front door and motioned the driver to continue around the mansion to the back entrance. Howard Hastings was waiting when the buggy arrived. The buggy stopped and the driver climbed down and opened the door to the enclosed vehicle.

"Mr. President! I'm honored! I had no idea it was you who was to visit me. Please come in quickly before you are seen.

"Mr. Hastings…"

"Howard please," said Hastings.

"Fine. Howard, it is good to see you again. I think it has been about six months since I saw you last."

"You're right, Mr. President. I recall you were in the adjoining box at Fifth Avenue Theater. We were both there to see *Jezebel*."

"Yes, the play by Dion Boucicault. What a good memory you have, Howard."

"Wow!" remarked Hastings. "I recalled the play but could never have come up with the playwright."

"Well, as it turns out, I'm a bit of a theater buff. Mrs. Grant and I enjoy getting to the theater every chance we get. And we have found we have a bit more anonymity if we take in plays in New York City as opposed to Washington DC."

"I must say I have never considered how difficult it must be to go out in public when a person is as well known as you."

"As I recall, Howard, there were several people greeting you as we left the theater."

"True, Mr. President. I am known by some in New York but I don't have nearly the reputation you do."

Hastings continued leading the president into his study and closed the door. Both men took seats. It was obvious to both of them that important business was to take place. Anticipation of that business blocked out thoughts of any other concerns.

"Howard, that brings me to why I wanted to see you. I have known you for a number of years and believe you to be a man of the highest integrity."

"Thank you, Mr. President. I'm honored that you believe that."

"Don't be honored. I'm not here to pay you a compliment. I'm here because I desperately need your help. Our country needs your help."

"I'll do what I can, sir. But I must say I'm at a loss as to how someone like me can help you or our country."

Just then there was a gentle knock at the door and Alvelda entered pushing a small cart. "I'm sorry to disturb you gentlemen but I thought you might like some refreshments. I have some little sandwiches I made with some leftovers and a pot of coffee." She pushed the cart over so the President could make his selections.

"Mr. President," said Howard. "I don't know if you met Alvelda as you came in. She is responsible for keeping things in order around here—and for making sure I have plenty of nourishment."

The President rose from his chair as he chewed and bowed slightly. He had a partial sandwich in one hand. "Miss Alvelda, I have to say I have never had a meatloaf sandwich. This is the most wonderful sandwich I have ever had."

"Thank you, Mr. President. Please excuse me while I let myself out." Alvelda left her cart, retreated from the room, and closed the door.

"As I was saying," said the President. "I'm here because I need your help—that is our country needs your help. First, I need to give you some background. You remember about three years ago when two scoundrels named Gould and Fisk set out to corner the gold market."

"Of course. I couldn't believe it was possible for two men to create such havoc. I was even caught up temporarily in the gold fever and bought a few thousand dollars in gold bullion in hopes of making a quick profit."

"Oh really," said the President. "How did you do?"

"I'm ashamed to say that I lost more than half of my original investment," said Hastings as he lowered his head in shame.

"Was it your own money or were you investing the railroad's money?"

"It was my money. I didn't want to risk the railroad's money before I knew if gold was a good investment."

"Howard, your desire to protect the railroad while taking a personal risk is one of the reasons I've come to you. As you recall, there was a long investigation after those scalawags tried to implicate me in their scheme."

"But you were cleared, sir. The whole country knows you didn't have anything to do with their underhanded dealings."

"Legally, I was cleared. I was found to be innocent of any wrongdoing. However, my association with them as they concocted their scheme, brought a cloud on my administration. I will never be free of the mark those men have put on my reputation. And Howard, there are other corrupt politicians like Boss Tweed that continue to cause citizens to question not just politicians but also the government."

"I can understand that," said Hastings. "Rather than let each person rise or fall on his or her own merits, some people find it easier to form quick judgments and prejudices. Just tell me how I can help you and it would be my privilege to do so."

"Howard, I've come to you because you probably know more about the railroad industry than any other person."

"You honor me, sir," said Hastings. "I don't believe I live up to your evaluation of me but I'm honored."

"What I believe is we're facing a crisis in our country that may have the railroads at its center."

"What crisis are you talking about? I can't think of anything that's going on in the railroad industry that's a threat to the country. That is, unless you're talking about the speculative quick expansion of some of the companies."

"That's exactly what I am talking about. Howard, I believe we're headed for a financial crisis that will threaten the stability of the country."

"I haven't heard anything about it," said Hastings. "But to be candid, I haven't had much time to think about what's been happening with the overall railroad business and around the country."

"And why is that?" asked the President.

"It seems Great National Railroad has somehow been taken over and I have just found out that I am no longer the CEO of the company."

"I'm sorry to hear that. Do you mind me asking what happened?"

"Mr. President, I'm glad to tell you but I don't see how my problems could be nearly as important as the concerns that brought you here."

"That's where you may be wrong," said the President. "Your problems may also be a part of the larger problem that is plaguing our country."

"I don't see how. But here is what has happened. I have been the CEO of Great National since John Crudder sold the company a few years ago. Before that, I was the second in responsibility for more than thirty years under his father, Robert. Unfortunately, Robert Crudder and his wife were killed in a buggy accident and John took over. I supported John as I had his father for so many years.

"But John's heart was not in the railroad business. He sold the company, went to law school, and headed out west to make a new life for himself. I fact, I have just contacted him and implored him to come home and help me figure out what to do. I sent the telegram to him just five days ago. I'm sure he's on his way but it will take him about two more weeks to get here."

"How have you been pushed out of your own company?" asked the President.

"Some of my rivals—actually I guess you could call them my enemies—got together and purchased just over half of the company's stock. The next thing I knew, they marched into my office, told me to leave and padlocked the door. They even had two policemen with them to ensure I didn't cause any trouble.

"They didn't have to worry about that. I'm not a fighter. I left quietly and contacted John and asked him to come give me some guidance."

"What do you think John will be able to do?"

"I'm not sure what anyone can do, Mr. President. But I have confidence if anyone can help me it would be John. He has a way of solving problems—sometimes doing it in secret—that seems to elude others. When he gets here, I think he'll find a way to once again take control of his father's empire."

"Then it seems like John Crudder is the man I really need to see. Do you think he would be willing to help me find a way to keep the railroads from ruining the economy of our nation?"

"Mr. President, I'm sure you can count on John to do whatever is within his power to help you."

"Well then, Howard," said the President as he stood and extended his hand. "My business is finished for today. Would you mind if I came calling about this same time two weeks from today? From what you told me, Crudder should be here by then."

"It would be my honor, Mr. President. And I'm sure John will also be happy to meet with you."

"Then it's settled. Until then, I bid you adieu." With those words the President walked out of the study and was met by the butler to escort him to the back door where he retrieved his hat and cane. He climbed into the closed buggy, briefly waved at Howard Hastings and lowered the window shade.

Roy Clinton

CHAPTER 5

I was watching from the train window as the train from Kansas pulled into Grand Central Depot. Curiously, I was not able to see anything. The last time I was in New York City, the Depot had been under construction but was not yet open. It was built for three independent railroad companies—Great National was not among them. Each railroad had separate waiting rooms, ticketing operations, and baggage handling.

The new terminal was a great step forward for New York. It was built on a large tract of land well north of the main business district in Lower Manhattan. In fact, I thought 42nd Street seemed remote and too far away from the heart of commerce. I then realized the train lines came into the terminal underground. No wonder I couldn't see anything from the train window. From the outside, the depot building didn't even look like it had anything to do with railroads. William Wilgus, the engineer responsible for the design of the terminal, even came up with the idea that the area above the tracks could be leased to developers. Already companies were lining up to buy what was referred to as "air rights" so they could build their offices, hotels, and restaurant adjacent to the new railroad building which was actually above the train tracks. As I thought about that, I knew it wouldn't be long until 42nd Street would be part of the sprawling commercial district.

I disembarked from the train and walked into the terminal building. As I got to the main lobby, I stopped at a large painting of my father. It was larger than life size and reminded me of how huge my father looked to me when I was a little boy. Beside the painting was a plaque that briefly told the history of Great National Railroad and of my father's philanthropic work in New York City. I stood mesmerized by the tribute. The porter who was following with my trunk stopped and waited patiently for me until I was ready to move on.

Outside the depot, I hired a buggy to take me to the Fifth Avenue Hotel. Walking into the regal building, I was flooded with emotion. The last time I was here was for my parents' funeral. They had been killed while I was finishing my studies at Harvard University.

"May I help you, sir? Sir... Sir!"

Still deep in my thoughts, I realized the clerk was talking to me. "I'm sorry. What did you say?"

"I asked if I could help you," said the clerk.

"Yes, I would like a suite please. I'm not sure how long I'll be here. I'm certain I will be here for a week but it may be a month or longer."

"We do have the Crudder Suite available," said the clerk. "It is the second finest suite in the hotel after the Presidential Suite."

"What did you call it?" I asked thinking surely my mind was playing tricks on me.

"The Crudder Suite. During a bit of renovation, we decided to rename the suite for Robert Crudder and his wife Lucille. He was the owner of Great National Railroad. Tragically, both of them were killed in a buggy accident not far from our front door. We thought it was fitting that we name the suite for the Crudders. They did so much for the city."

"I think I would rather have another suite please." The idea of occupying a suite named for my parents brought another round of great sadness. I was sure if I stayed there I would continually be distracted from my true business in New York which was to regain control of the railroad my father had built.

"I'm sorry, sir. I'm afraid that is all we have available."

"Then I'll take the Presidential Suite," I said feeling sure it would not be occupied.

"That too is occupied, sir," replied the clerk. "I'm indeed sorry but President Grant himself is in residence. We always have the suite available for him when he is in the city."

"Fine then, I'll take the Crudder Suite." I resigned myself to the fact that for some reason, I was destined not only to be surrounded by the memory of my parents, but I was going to be immersed in those memories for my entire stay in the city.

"May I have your name, sir?" The clerk asked with pen poised above the registration form.

"It's Crudder. John Crudder."

"Oh my. Are you kin to Robert and Lucille Crudder?"

"I am. They were my parents," I replied.

"I'm so very sorry, sir. I can understand your reticence in wanting to occupy that suite. If you will give me an hour, I'm sure the manager can prevail on one of the other guests to exchange suites with you."

"That won't be necessary," I said. "I'll be glad to take the suite. I was just shocked when I heard you had named a suite for my parents. Please thank the management for their sentiment."

"I'll be glad to do so, sir. Do you have any luggage?

"Yes. I have a trunk the bellman is just unloading."

"I'll have it sent up to your suite right away," said the clerk. "And we do have conveniences in your room. You have a water closet and your own bathtub. Only your suite and the Presidential Suite are so equipped."

"That sounds fine," I said as I reflected on my childhood home as having the same luxuries. I knew Mr. Hastings would have allowed me to stay there but I opted for the hotel so I wouldn't be plunged so deeply into memories that were still painful. But it seems my time in New York City will also be the time for me to work through the pain of losing my parents.

"We have two new Otis elevators," the clerk said with pride that couldn't be greater if he had paid for the elevators himself. "If you will step this way, you will be escorted to your room and your trunk will be brought up shortly."

I paused at the door of the suite and read the brass plaque.

The
CRUDDER SUITE
In Memory of Robert and Lucille Crudder

Tears formed in my eyes in spite of my attempt not to let them. A bellman unlocked the door and began explaining the features of the room. I was aware he was speaking but I didn't hear what he said. He opened the windows that overlooked Fifth Avenue. I tipped him a dollar and walked to the windows. Looking down at the street, I relived the horrible moment the president of Harvard told me my parents had been killed. Then I had a picture in my mind of the fire engine speeding by and my parents' buggy being upended. But until now, I didn't know the location of the accident.

I must have stood at the window for half an hour just looking at the street below. Did my parents know what was happening to them? Did they suffer?

When I collected my emotions and turned from the window, I saw my trunk sitting at the foot of the bed. Evidently I was so lost in thought I was not even aware when it was brought in. I unpacked the trunk and hung up my suits, shirts, and topcoat. Although I was eager to see Mr. Hastings, I knew I needed a bath. I went back down to the front desk and arranged for hot water to be brought to my room and for my suits and shirts to be pressed. After my bath, I dressed in a suit and told myself I needed to be conscious to subdue my Texas accent as much as possible.

Howard Hastings was back at his Fifth Avenue mansion, the home I grew up in, for he had been locked out of his office at Great National Railroad about three weeks before. He recalled me telling him that when he sold the company it was with the proviso that he was the CEO for life. I could only imagine his confusion at being thrown out of the company he ran.

I arrived at the home about midday. All I knew was Howard said he had been fired and the company was at risk of being taken over. I rang the bell and waited. Alvelda opened the door and threw her arms around me. "Johnny! Oh Johnny, let me look at you. It seems married life has been agreeing with you. I think you have put on a few pounds." My childhood nanny poked me in the ribs and then hugged me again. "Come on in. I know Mr. Hastings has been expecting you. I'll tell him you're here. I just can't get over how much you have changed since your wedding. You are looking more like your father every day."

I was stunned. No one had ever told me I resembled my father. But then the only people from New York I have had much contact with are Howard and Alvelda. I took in Alvelda's words and realized I was sad thinking how I missed my parents. Their buggy accident had cut their lives short and thrust me into adulthood before I wanted. Memories of childhood flooded my mind. Mostly sad ones. I didn't have many friends as a child so Alvelda was my playmate. She did her best to make up for the loneliness I felt. I was always small for my age and was picked on regularly. Dear Alvelda gave me the confidence I needed to compete with others and to do my best in school. She picked me up when I fell and encouraged me to try again.

It's interesting that I was not only small for my age as a child, but now in adulthood, I am still shorter than any other man I know. At just over five feet tall, I was the brunt of bullying until I learned to defend myself with my fists and later with guns and knives. It has been a long time since I have felt at a disadvantage because of my short stature but seeing Alvelda brought all of those old feelings back.

"John!" shouted Mr. Hastings as he entered the parlor. "Thank you so much for coming. Lots has happened since I saw you last. I have so much to tell you. I don't know where to start."

"Hello, Howard. It's so good to see you!"

"And it's so good to see you, John. You sound even more Texan than you did at your wedding. How long ago was that? Has it been two years?"

"Near about," I said. Pulling the tintypes from my coat pocket, I proudly showed Howard. "Here are Charlotte and the girls. That's Claire on the left and Cora on the right. At least I think that's right. I still have trouble telling them apart."

"Thankfully they look just like their mother," said Howard as he pointed at the likeness of my family and laughed.

"You're shor right about that."

"It looks like they have their mother's blond hair," Howard said.

"They do indeed. And they both have her blue eyes. They're

just a little over a year old. And Howard, they both started walking when they were just over nine months old. One day they were crawling and then Clare stood up and took a few steps. Just a few minutes later Cora stood up and they both laughed. You should see them. They're into everything. Now they walk all over the house and talk to each other and laugh. Charlotte and I can only understand a few words but they seem to understand everything the other says. I met some ladies on the stagecoach who are twins and they said twins develop their own vocabulary. They called it twin language."

"I'm so happy for you," Howard said. "Let's go into the study so I can fill you in on what has been going on."

I followed Howard into the study. Alvelda brought in coffee and cookies and then closed the door so we could visit in private.

"John, I've been removed from the company. I don't know how they did it or why, but I have been fired and as I told you in the telegram, I think the company has been sold, or maybe stolen by unscrupulous men."

"Howard don't worry about it. I'll see that this is all set right. They can't fire you and they can't sell the company. I have a lot to tell you as well."

"That's fine, John. I want to hear all about it. But I need to tell you that we're going to have a visitor sometime today. I'm not sure what all is going on but...."

Just then there was a knock on the back door. Howard opened the door to the sitting room and called to Alvelda, "I'll get it, Alvelda. I think the caller is for me." Howard went to the door and opened it. By now, you know the visitor was the President of the United States.

***

"But I don't understand, Mr. President. How could you have known I was even in town?" I asked the President.

"John, don't you think I have the resources to gain the knowledge I need for any situation?" said President Grant laughing as he pulled a cigar from his coat pocket. "Mr. Hastings is it alright if I smoke?" asked the President as he lit his cigar.

"Of course, Mr. President, you may smoke in my house," said Hastings. In a few moments the President had produced a great cloud of smoke that virtually filled the room. Then he turned to me and continued his conversation.

"What was it you asked? Oh yes, how had I known you were in town. I thought there was a good chance you'd be staying at the Fifth Avenue Hotel so I asked the building management to notify me immediately when you checked in. It seems you had your trunk delivered, had a bath, and your clothes pressed."

I stood silently as I realized Mr. Grant was a very resourceful man. My mind was spinning as I wondered just how much the President really knew about my work as the Midnight Marauder. I wondered if I had made mistakes and somehow not protected my identity as carefully as I thought.

"So, John, you see if I can find out when you take a bath, do you think it would be that difficult for me to know something about what has been going on in Bandera, Texas, and about your role in it?"

I did my best not to express any kind of alarm but I could tell my face was flushed. How had I slipped up? Where had I made mistakes?

"Now, now, John. Don't be concerned. I'm not here to cause you trouble. As I have indicated, I need your help. It is just that Governor Davis is a close friend of mine. He and I served together during the war. I sure wish there was something more I could do for Governor Davis. It looks like he'll be defeated in the election coming up in a few weeks.

"But that is neither here nor there. What was I saying? Oh yes, I was getting ready to talk about the Midnight Marauder. It seems the Midnight Marauder never appeared until you had left Bandera, supposedly to come to New York to assist your deceased parents. There's good evidence the Midnight Marauder was instrumental, if not personally responsible, in the removal of the entire corrupt town council. Now I don't condone violence during peacetime but I think the Midnight Marauder did the State of Texas a favor by ridding the state of such corrupt politicians. Such people give politics a bad name."

"I'm not sure what to say, Mr. President," I said trying to come up with some explanation, excuse, or denial—and not knowing which I should employ. "It's true, I used a ruse to leave Bandera. I didn't want to remain as marshal in the town with the leaders being involved in crime. But if you think I know anything about…"

"Just hold on, John. I'm not here to accuse you or to cause you any harm. Let's just say I pride myself on gathering the intelligence I need to do my job. And if it was possible to do so I would like to shake the hand of the Midnight Marauder and thank him for his service to our nation. But since I can't do that, I would like to just shake your hand. May I do that, John?"

The President held out his hand and I reluctantly took it. He had a firm handshake that bordered on being painful. I looked up into his eyes and said, "I'm proud to shake your hand, Mr. President." The President was considerably shorter than most other men but still he towered over me. He continued shaking my hand for several seconds before he released it and went back to puffing his cigar.

"Now let's get down to business, John. Let me tell you the problems I'm having and how I think you can help."

Over the next few minutes, the President told me of the panic that had gripped New York and also *persuaded* me to help bring that panic under control. As I accepted the President's offer to help with the current financial crisis, I did make one stipulation.

"Mr. President, it will be an honor for me to be of service to my country," I said, "And I'm sure the Midnight Marauder will feel that way as well. However, the Midnight Marauder's true identity must never become known. And I know the only way he will accept the assignment is for him to be able to freely take actions he believes are necessary. I can tell you I know he always operates inside of the law unless he feels the only way he can accomplish his purpose is to go outside the law."

"John, that's fine. I'll accept those conditions. I trust you and the Midnight Marauder will get to the bottom of what is going on in the railroad industry and be able to stop the panic that has consumed New York City and prevent our nation from being plunged into depression."

"I will do my best, Mr. President. And I know the Midnight Marauder will as well."

"Well, I guess that concludes my business here," said the President. "Howard, thank you for setting up this meeting for me. Gentlemen, please come see me in Washington DC at the Executive Mansion when you have news to report. And John, I'm counting on you. I hope you will not let us down."

"I will do my best, sir," I said. "I hope it will be enough."

"If you give your best," came the President's reply, "I can't ask for more than that."

With those words, President Ulysses S. Grant left the mansion, entered his closed carriage waiting on the drive behind the house, and drove away.

CHAPTER 6

Back in Bandera, Slim was true to his word and ramped up his role from grandpa to that of stand-in father. Charlotte was in her element as a mother. The twins kept her busy, and she loved every minute of her time with them. But it was also nearly more than she could handle.

Slim continued his practice of coming over for coffee each morning. He learned what helped Charlotte most was coming over early with his coffee and rocking on the porch until he heard one of the twins stirring. He would then slip inside, retrieve the baby that was awake, and return to the porch.

Most mornings, he realized when one baby was awake, the other woke up, too. When that happened he picked up both granddaughters and carried them out to his rocker. He found the twins were seldom fussy. When they awoke, they were ready to play and ready to eat. He couldn't help in the eating department but he did enjoy rocking them and talking back to their gibberish.

When Charlotte woke up, she would retrieve both girls, take them back to her bedroom and feed them while Slim put on a pot of coffee and cooked breakfast. Although Charlotte missed John, she had to admit that she loved the time she spent with her father. It reminded her so much of her own childhood and how she would jump at the chance to spend all available time with him.

Twice a week, Slim would head into town after breakfast. His election as mayor necessitated he get into town on occasion, if for no other reason than to be seen and let the town's people know their mayor was on the job. There was still a mayor's office and if nothing else was going on, after he walked through town and visited with the proprietors, he would pick up his mail and drop by his seldom used office to read any letters he received. Usually, before noon, he would head back to the H&F to join Charlotte and the girls for the noon meal. On one of his morning trips to town, Marshall Williams dropped by for a visit.

"Mornin' Clem. To what do I owe the pleasure?"

"Mornin' Mayor."

"Now Clem, when are you goin' to go back to calling me Slim?"

"I'm sorry, Slim. It's just that I more often think of you as the mayor of Bandera than I do as my friend Slim."

"But I'm both, Clem."

"I know you are. I just forget."

"Always glad to see you. Now did you come by to get another cup of my coffee? Lord knows, no one, including you, can tolerate your coffee. Or did you come by as Marshal on town business?"

"Well, I guess a little of both." Clem grinned as he helped himself to Slim's coffee pot. "You're shor right about my coffee. I never could make it so it tasted like somethin' I wanted to drink. But I make it anyway and drink what I can. Once in a while, someone will stop by the office and get a cup. Course when they do, I have to listen to how it's the worst coffee they ever drank. Not that I care much but I do wish I wasn't known as havin' the worst coffee in town. Maybe you could give me lessons, Slim. If I could make coffee like you, that would be one less thing for people to laugh at me for."

"Clem, people don't laugh at you," said Slim.

"Yes, they do and you know it. Maybe they don't laugh as much as they once did but they still remember the boneheaded things I did when I was deputy. And when anyone walks in my office, I hear cracks like, 'I see you're awake, Marshal.'"

"Clem, I know people sometimes make fun of you. But you know their respect for you runs deep. Shor some like to kid you. Don't let it get to you. Now Marshal, I've got a feelin' you didn't come over here just to jaw about coffee. What can I do for you?"

"You're right about that," said Clem. "Old man Barlow came in and said someone has stolen nigh onto thirty head of his cattle."

"What? I didn't know we had any cattle rustlin' in Bandera since the old town council was put out of business."

"Well we don't have a lot," said Marshal Williams. "But 'bout every week, someone stops by and tells me they've lost some cattle. Most times they are missin' one or two head. But Red Nichols has been in a couple of times complainin' that someone has taken his cattle. It's never many but he does complain and asks me what I'm gonna do 'bout it.''

"So what are you gonna do, Marshal?" asked Slim.

"I'm not rightly shor what to do. It's not like I can investigate every time someone has a cow run off. But this is different. Barlow don't never cause any problems and he don't complain much. With him losing thirty head, I think I need to do somethin' but I'm not sure what."

"Did Barlow tell you if all of his cattle were branded?" asked Slim.

"Shor did. He said they were all branded. He raised all of them from calves and said he brands them soon after they drop."

"Do any of the other ranchers who complained of missin' cattle live near Barlow?"

"Red Nichols does," said Clem. "His land meets up with Barlow's. They both have pretty big spreads just west of town a few miles."

"Well Marshal, it sounds like you might want to get the cattleman's association involved."

"You're right!" said Clem. "I never thought of that but that's what they're for. I'll bet none of them know about the losses of other ranchers. I'll get some signs posted around town. You reckon a week is enough time to get word out about a meetin'?"

"I think it should be. I can stop by a couple of ranches later today and tell the m about the meeting when I'm headed back to the H&F."

Clem rubbed his chin. "And I'll ride out to old man Barlow's place and tell him 'bout the meetin' and then I can tell Red Nichols when I'm out that way."

"Clem, keep in mind that no one expects the marshal to keep track of every head of cattle in the county. But by gettin' the cattle owners together, you can appeal to them to share their knowledge and look for a solution."

"You're shor right again Slim. I'll get those signs up and start notifyin' ranchers this afternoon. By the way, has the H&F been missin' any cattle?"

"Nothin' like Barlow. We occasionally have a head or two wander off. But with our operation, it's difficult to know if any cattle are missin' unless we find signs of rustlin' and we haven't seen any. And you can be certain we watch closely for that since losing so many head a couple of years ago."

"Do you think there could be rustlin' happenin' on a smaller scale?" asked Clem.

Slim paused for a moment, cocked his head to the side indicating he was considering Clem's suggestion. "Marshal, I've never thought about it before, but you might be on to somethin'. I always considered rustlin' would take place on a larger scale, like what Barlow has experienced. But I never considered when a rancher was missin' just a head or two that rustlin' might be involved."

Clem stood straighter and got a bit of a smile on his face. "Thanks, Slim. Maybe I'm not as much of the town joke as some people think I am."

"You remember that, Marshal. If we do have a rustlin' problem, you're the one who put the pieces together and discovered it. Go ahead and get your signs up and we'll both start gettin' the word out about the meetin'."

"And Clem. If you have a few more minutes, I'll tell you what I know about coffee."

The marshal's face brightened. "I shor do, Slim. Tell me what to do."

"First thing you do is to go over to the mercantile and get some Arbuckle Ariosa Coffee. It has a yellow label with a flying angel on the front of the package and big red letters. They always keep some because they order it for the H&F and we use a lot of it. It costs a little more but I think it's worth it."

"What's so special 'bout it?" asked Clem.

"Well, you still roast your coffee beans in a skillet on the stove in your office, don't you?"

"Just like my grandmother taught me when I was a little boy," said Clem with a smile on his face.

"Well the Arbuckle brothers roast the beans for you using an egg and sugar glaze. That seals in the flavor and the good coffee smell. Then all you have to do is to grind it before you make a pot. There's even a piece of peppermint candy inside each package."

"So that's all there is to it?" asked Clem.

"No. That just gets you started. I've watched you make coffee, Clem. You pour a handful of coffee grounds into your pot, add water, let it boil, and then drink it. But you've got it backwards. First you boil your water and then move the pot back away from the fire so the water is not as hot. Then you add two spoons of coffee for every cup of water. Stir the grounds into the water. Wait two minutes and stir again. Then you wait another two minutes and sprinkle some cold water into the pot to settle the grounds."

"That's how you made this coffee?" Clem asked as he held up his cup.

"Yup. Then one other thing. When your coffee is made, pour it slowly into the cup so as not to disturb the grounds in the bottom of the pot."

A big grin spread across the marshal's face. "I'll bet I can make coffee as good as you now."

"I'm sure you can, Clem. And you can keep the secret. A cook on the H&F taught me about five years ago. But you have to have Arbuckle coffee and you need to make it like I told you. If you do, it will come out tasting good might near every time."

"I'm sure indebted to you, Slim. And I'll keep your secret." The marshal stood and set his empty cup over on the desk. "Well, I better mosey on over to the printin' office and get some signs made. I'll see you at the cattleman's meetin' next week."

"I'll be there, Marshal."

Slim mounted his horse and rode slowly back to the ranch. On the way he pondered what Clem had asked about whether rustlers could be working in Bandera. The more he thought about it, the more it sounded like the marshal was onto something. Even small spreads wouldn't think of rustling if they only lost one or two head. And larger ranches wouldn't notice if five or ten head went missing.

When Slim got to the H&F, he went to see his foreman. Owen was in the dining hall just finishing his meal. Slim sat down with Owen and told him about the conversation he had with the marshal.

Owen contemplated Slim's words as he chewed his food. "Slim, I never thought about it before but I think you could be right. I've had several of the hands mention they thought a head or two was missin'. I don't pay much attention to it if it is just one or two head. They usually turn up and the hands seldom report when that happens. I'll start keepin' closer track of the reports. Over time, a small loss here and there could turn into something bigger. But I haven't seen anything suspicious around the ranch. And no one has reported any strangers. Sure, there are riders that come through on occasion, but they generally just ride on through and don't cause no harm."

"Thanks, Owen. Keep as careful a tally as you can. If there's rustlin' goin' on, I want to know it so we can put a stop to it now!"

"I'll do that," said Owen.

CHAPTER 7

Howard, I don't know what I am supposed to do or where to start. Tell me what's been going on. And try not to leave out any details. I must have the whole story if I am gonna be able to help."

"Well, it started a little over a year ago," Howard said. "I was in my office one day when a delegation of stock holders knocked on the door of my office."

"How did they get past your secretary?" I asked.

"They just barged on past her. As she was getting up to greet them, one put a heavy hand on her shoulder and pushed her back down and said, 'We know the way. We don't need your help.'"

"They knocked twice but before I could get up, they came in and fanned out around my desk. Then a self-important man named Buckminster Carmichael stood right in front of my desk and stuck out his chest and waited for the others to take their places. He hooked his thumbs in his vest and in a voice much louder than necessary said, 'Mr. Hastings, we don't like the way you've been running Great National. We're here to serve you notice that we want some changes made and if you don't make 'em, you'll be out of a job.'"

"Did they say what they wanted to change?" I asked.

"Not really. John, I've gone back and listened to that conversation in my head many times since that day and the only thing really clear to me is they wanted me out but couldn't seem to land on something I'd done they didn't like. They talked about stock prices and about the expansion of other railroads. Another man with Carmichael also had lots to say. His name is William Summerall. Summerall and Carmichael both had many critical words for your father, or who they called 'Old man Crudder.' That really got my hackles up. They can criticize me all they want. But your father was the best at what he did. I have my shortcomings, but your father had no equals in this industry."

"I appreciate you saying that, Howard. But don't sell yourself short. I haven't been watching too closely but I've been keeping up with the company—at least somewhat. And your job is secure. While it's true that I sold a large part of Great National, I didn't sell nearly all of it.

"The company is so large that when I sold the block of stock, it seems everyone assumed that was the entire company. After that it was just a matter of structuring the sale so it had the appearance of the whole company. The language I put in the documents I prepared at the sale, particularly around you being the CEO for life helped complete my charade. It was assumed I was selling the entire company since I added that provision. I never told the group of investors I was selling the whole railroad. I simply said I found out I wasn't cut out to follow in my father's footsteps and would rather pursue other interests."

"John, I still can't believe you still own the railroad."

"I'm sorry about deceiving you, Howard. I just knew I still had some growing up to do before I could completely let go of what my father had built. I was having a hard time figuring out what I wanted to do. Studying business, then law, then being a cowhand and then a marshal. I was searching for my way in life and didn't want my father's company to be a casualty of my youth."

"You said you had been keeping up with the company," said Hastings. "How were you doing that?"

"From time to time, I'd get a copy of the *New York Times* when I was in Austin or San Antonio. I enjoyed reading about things in New York and especially any mention of Great National. And I've spent a significant amount of time in Fort Worth. I keep a room there and have a subscription to the *Times* delivered year-round. Any time I'm back in Fort Worth, I go through the stack of newspapers and am able to catch up quickly on all of the railroad business. I also follow stock prices—especially of Great National.

"But Howard, back to Summerall and Carmichael," I said. "What happened next?"

"Well, the next month was the annual shareholder's meeting. John, those meetings are always routine and even boring. We've never had more than maybe twenty or thirty people present. Your father would call the meetings to order and go through the formalities. He would have me read a report about the highlights of the year. Our accountant would bring his report. Then your father would stand and bring the meeting to a close. It never lasted over half an hour." Howard paused and reached for a glass of water, took several swallows, and then continued.

"John, I've been in more than twenty annual shareholder's meetings and they always were conducted in the same manner. Well, I knew things were going to be different when I arrived early to the annual meeting and found the room was already full and overflowing into the hall. There must have been two hundred people there. Each had the credentials that showed they were stockholders, though most owned ten shares or less and many owned only a single share. I realized Summerall and Carmichael were behind this and they had bought the participation of most of the crowd by giving them one share of stock. At least I think that's what they did."

"So what happened at the meeting," I asked, trying to hurry Howard along.

"When I stood to call the meeting to order, several people shouted at once demanding the right to speak. I regained control and tried to move the meeting forward but every few minutes I was interrupted by someone else who wanted to speak. Finally, I relented and called on a few of the people to speak. Each person who came to the podium had a prepared speech. All of them said about the same thing and even sounded like they were written by the same person."

"From what you've told me, they probably were," I said. "Summerall or Carmichael or both."

"I'm sure you are correct, John. Anyway they kept using terms like, 'grievous errors' and 'malfeasance' and saying I have been 'derelict in my duties as chief executive officer.' They even presented a petition supposedly signed by five hundred shareholders calling for my dismissal as CEO. Well, by that time, I had all that I could take. I ruled the petition out of order and said all the business at hand had been taken care of and I ended the meeting.

"I've never been around so many angry people. They shouted at me and called me names and continued to besmirch your father's good name. I pushed through the crowd to get back to my office. On my way out several made threats to me and kicked me and several shoved me, almost knocking me down. And as I was going out the door, one man I've never seen before spit in my face. Try as I might I couldn't come up with anything I'd done to deserve that treatment. By that time, I was in fear of my safety. I never did anything to any of those people. I even called Alan Pinkerton in Chicago and asked if he could provide security for me.

"A few days later some of the same group barged into my office and Summerall told me I was fired and had policemen escort me from the building."

"Howard, I had no idea you've been going through such a trial. I wish you'd have let me know earlier."

"I would have if I thought there was anything you could have done. You were so far away I thought the best thing I could do was to make sure my family and I were protected. We've had security present ever since that shareholder's meeting."

"You did the right thing," I told Howard as I put a hand on his shoulder.

"John, I still can't make sense of any of it. The company's always done well and, at the risk of sounding immodest, the past two years have been the most profitable in our history."

"You're right in that. I followed the stock prices carefully. And my shadow corporation directors carefully watched what was going on with the part of Great National you managed and made sure the rest of the company paralleled your decisions. You have been an outstanding manager."

"Then why have so many people been angry with me?" Howard asked.

"From what you've said," I began, "Summerall and Carmichael wanted control of the railroad and they needed to get you out of the way. You said you thought they bought off the participation of the crowd at the meeting by giving them each a single share of stock and then arming them with speeches written for them. And they no doubt incited the anger that has been vented at you."

"John, that's exactly what happened. While I've always known that, I still have had this nagging feeling I was not doing a good job. Why else would so many people—hundreds of people—be so upset with me?"

"You mentioned you got Pinkerton to provide security. How

did that work out?"

"Well, they have an office in New York, so Pinkerton quickly assigned two guards around the clock, one covering me and one covering my wife."

"No, I mean, were the guards effective? Did it turn out you needed them?" I asked.

"I'll say I did. Just a few weeks after the meeting, someone tried to burn down the Fifth Avenue mansion. My wife and I have both had several death threats. Employees of the company have been harassed. There was even an attempt to disrupt rail service on several of our lines. I think all of it goes back to Summerall and Carmichael."

I was stunned as I listened to Howard tell me of the troubles he had faced over the past year. He continued telling me of having to hire more Pinkerton detectives and guards to try to get to the bottom of the efforts to stop the progress of Great National. Even with the considerable resources of the Pinkerton Agency, no solid proof was found that pointed back to Summerall and Carmichael.

"They even tried to bribe me," Howard continued.

"Who did?"

"I'm not certain but I think it had to be Summerall and Carmichael."

"Tell me what happened, Howard. I want it all."

"Well, a messenger delivered a package that contained a letter saying I was going to be given instructions on how to run Great National. And if I did as I was told, I would receive another package like that every year for the rest of my life."

"What was in the package?"

"John, there were twenty, five thousand dollar bills!"

"What? One hundred thousand dollars?" I couldn't believe what I was hearing.

"Obviously this group had some very significant financial backing. What did you do with the money?" I asked as I wondered what the most appropriate thing was to do under the circumstances.

"I immediately reported it to Edward King. He's the president of the New York Stock Exchange. I also gave King the money. He called a meeting of the Exchange and reported the bribery attempt and asked what the members knew about it. Of course I was at the meeting since you saw to it that I got the seat that was once occupied by your father. No one claimed to have any knowledge of it. After that, I was sure I was going to be receiving other letters giving me instructions and telling me to do outrageous things with the company but that was the last I heard. No one has attempted to contact me since. It has made me wonder if the person who sent the letter was a member of the Exchange."

"I wouldn't be at all surprised," I said.

"Well, John, guess who was sitting right across the aisle from me during the meeting?"

"Summerall and Carmichael," I said as Howard nodded his head. "I didn't realize they had seats on the exchange. In fact, I had never heard of their names until you told me about them.

What kind of business are they in?"

"Well, they are both stockbrokers now but I think Summerall started out in banking. I'm not sure what Carmichael did before becoming a broker. He may have always been a broker, so far as I know." Howard continued, "So two good things came out of the bribery attempt. First, the person or persons who were attempting to bribe me immediately gave up their intentions when knowledge of their actions became known. The second thing is the Exchange voted the money would be returned to me in a year to do with as I pleased. In fact, the exchange just returned the same bills I turned into them. They're in the safe. I'm going to put them back into the company."

"Yes, those are both good things. But Howard, after what you have gone through during the past year, I think the money should go to you. I believe you've earned it by your honesty and integrity as well as by the trauma you've endured."

"Well I never intended for that money to be for me. It's not mine."

"I say it is. And since you now know I own the controlling interest in the company, I guess that means I get to make that decision," I said with a smile on my face.

Howard looked toward the floor and said, "John, I don't know how to express my feelings right now. You've seen to it that I'll never have any financial concerns. Now to have this money come to me, it leaves me humbled and not certain about how to proceed." Howard was silent for several seconds as he gathered his thoughts.

"As I said earlier, John, I don't have any financial needs. In fact, I have more than enough money to last a lifetime and still leave a fortune to my children—if I don't give it away before then. What I'd like to do is to ask your permission to divide the money among the employees and give it to them in a few weeks as a Christmas bonus."

"I think that would be a fine idea," I told Howard. "But I think you need to make it clear that this was an unusual event not to be repeated. I would not want them to think every year they'll get that kind of windfall at Christmas."

"That's right. I need to make that clear," Howard said with a laugh. "They have been just fine with the five percent bonus we've always given at Christmas. We don't want them to expect such a large gift next year."

Howard continued to tell me what had transpired over the past year. When I thought I had heard the worst, he continued to surprise me with more low dealings by the ones who were set on taking control of the company.

"Then just a few months ago," said Howard, "I think it was about the middle or end of spring, rumors were being spread about Great National being involved in fraud. In fact, the rumors got such traction that I noticed the share price of our stock started to move downward. At first I was not concerned because it always moves up and down but the prevailing trend has always been upward. But this time, it started down and then continued to be on a downward slope."

"What did you do?" I asked.

"Well, I hurriedly called a board meeting to let the directors know what was going on and to seek their wisdom. We talked about doing several things but what we settled on was having our financial statement issued earlier than the end of the quarter and then planting a story with a reporter from the *Times*."

"Now things are making more sense to me. I saw the article in the *Times* that gave such a glowing report of the management of Great National and bragged that there was no company that had more integrity in how they conducted business. I was taken aback as I read the article but I couldn't figure what had brought it on. Good job, Howard! You have indeed proven that I left the right man in charge."

Howard bowed slightly and said, "I do thank you for your confidence. My desire has always been to conduct business the way your father would. I have often asked myself, 'What would Robert do in this situation?' I've found I was then able to make rather clearheaded decisions. I do appreciate knowing you're pleased with my leadership.

"Well, I wish I could say that was the end of the turmoil but it wasn't. They next accused me of fraud but those rumors soon died out, especially since they began right after the *Times* article came out. But then there were more threats made to me and my wife."

"What kind of threats?" I asked.

"They were mainly threats of physical harm. I wasn't too concerned since we had the protection of the Pinkerton Agency. But there was a very troubling thing that happened. My daughter discovered someone had killed her dog. It was bad enough they killed the poor thing but I was furious my daughter saw it. John, I'm glad I didn't come in contact with either Summerall or Carmichael then. I'm afraid I would have hurt them."

I was enraged as I listened. "Howard, I think the Midnight Marauder might eventually pay a visit to those men. And it's a good thing that visit is not now. For I think their lives would come to an abrupt end."

"John don't do anything rash. I don't want to see you get into any trouble."

"Don't worry about me. I get angry, but I've made it a point never to take action when I'm angry. Men who would do such a thing to a child are certainly capable of doing much worse. And I believe before long, we'll find they've been up to many more evil things.

"So what happened next?"

"I think you've heard about all of it," said Howard. "The next thing that happened was when they threw me out of my office a month ago. Once that happened, I immediately telegraphed you. Since then I have been moping around the house wondering what I did wrong and what I could have done to prevent what happened.

"Oh yes, then I got a telegram just a couple of days later telling me I would have a special visitor. As it turned out, that visitor was President Grant. He told me he needed my help. He also told me he needed your help. John, I want you to know I didn't tell him anything about the Midnight Marauder."

"Don't worry about that, Howard. I know you didn't. I was shocked when I thought the President knew of my secret identity. He didn't come out and say so but he certainly has his suspicions. But once I got over the shock, I realized he was not interested in harming me but was really seeking my assistance."

Roy Clinton

CHAPTER 8

This meetin' of the Bandera Cattleman's Association is called to order," shouted Barlow over the din in the meeting room above the Cheer Up Saloon. He rapped a glass against the table and slowly the forty or so men settled down and took their seats.

"As some of you already know, I didn't call this meetin'. The marshal did." There was a murmur as the members thought how unusual it was for the meeting not to be called by the association's president. "I was talkin' to the marshal last week and told him I was missin' about thirty head. He told me he would check into it. The next thing I knew, he had ridden out to my ranch and told me he was callin' a meeting of the Cattleman's Association. I don't have to tell you I thought he'd overstepped his authority a bit." Several members nodded their heads in agreement and began to murmur louder.

"Just listen to me now," said Barlow. "I said I 'thought' he overstepped his authority but I was wrong. When he told me why he called the meetin', I knew he'd done the right thing. He told me of several of you who've lost a few head of cattle and told me he was worried that rustlers might be movin' into Bandera again."

The noise level in the room rose and one of the men shouted, "We ain't got no rustlin' problem here. If we did, we'd all know it." Again several men nodded their heads as the man continued. "Nobody but you has lost many head. That's just the cattle business. Cows are dumb creatures who'll wander off and get lost." Again there was the sound of agreement in the room and more men nodded.

"Sure they are," said Barlow. "And I've just been thinkin' the same thing. The cattle I'm missin' have just wandered off. When I have time to go out and search for 'em, I was sure I would find 'em. But I want to ask you something. How many of you have had cattle missing over the past month?" Nearly every man raised a hand.

"So what if," asked Barlow, "your cattle didn't just wander off? What if someone took 'em just two or three head at a time so as not to worry you? Do you think there's a chance we might have a rustlin' problem?"

The murmur grew louder as the men considered the question of rustling in Bandera. The initial skepticism gave way to concern as they realized if rustlers had once again come to Bandera, no rancher was safe. Barlow held up his hands calling for quiet and once again addressed the room.

"I'd like the marshal to come up and tell you what he told me.

Clem, come tell us more about why you think there may be rustlers in Bandera."

Clem sauntered to the front of the room and took off his hat. "Howdy men." Several men said howdy in return. "I went over to see the mayor last week. I told Slim I knew several of you had lost some cattle. Red, I know you've lost several head."

"I think it's about seven or eight all told," said Red.

"Half a dozen of you have told me of losing one or two head over the last month," said Clem. "Then Barlow told me he thought he lost near thirty head. Anyway, when I was talkin' to Slim, he told me the H&F had a few losses, but he hadn't become concerned about it. But I asked him, what if some real slippery rustlers started workin' the ranches and not takin' lots of cattle but only one, two, or three head at a time? Slim, do you want to add anythin' to what I said?"

"Yes I do, Marshal," said Slim. "I realized you might have recognized a problem none of the rest of us did. And I think the marshal's right. We very well could have a team of rustlers workin' Bandera quietly so as not to raise suspicion. I think we owe Clem our thanks for bringin' this to our attention."

The room erupted in spontaneous applause as Slim sat down. The marshal continued to speak. "Thanks men. I 'preciate that. But back to business. How many of you have brought on new hires in the last two months?" More than half of the men raised a hand. "And you men with your hands in the air, how many of you have also lost cattle durin' the past two months?" Most of the hands stayed up. "Now, I have one more question," said the marshal. "How many of you who've not hired new hands have lost any cattle in the past two months?" Only two men raised their hands.

The murmur became much louder as the men contemplated what the marshal was laying out for them. "So Marshal, what do you suggest we do? Are you sayin' the new hires are stealin' our cattle?"

"Not at all," said Clem. "I'm just pointin' out rustlin' could be happenin' even if there aren't huge losses of cattle. Just because you're losing one or two head, doesn't mean the cattle were not stolen. And as far as the new hands go, I think we just need to be aware of any new people in our midst. We don't have to be suspicious, but I do think we should be watchful and not be too trustin' right off. And men, you need to talk to each other. When somethin' out of the ordinary happens on your ranch, you need to tell other ranchers. You're the first defense we have against someone stealin' your property."

Clem sat down and Barlow took his place. "You heard the marshal. If there's a problem with rustlin', the way to stop it is to talk to each other. And the way to keep our town from ever bein' taken over again by rustlers or crooked politicians, for that matter, is to keep talkin' to each other. If there's rustlin' goin' on, we'll find out and put a stop to it.

"Marshal, thanks for bringin' this to our attention," said Barlow. "And Marshal, anytime you think there needs to be a meetin' of the Cattleman's Association, you go ahead and call it. We'll all be obliged."

As the meeting broke up, several of the men came up to Clem and shook his hand. Others slapped him on the back and others just said "thanks" as they walked by. When all of the members had left except Slim, the marshal asked Slim how he felt the meeting went.

"Well, Marshal, no one was laughin' at you today. You may have called our attention to a problem we didn't know existed. We're fortunate to have you as our marshal."

Slim walked out of the room and went down the stairs as the marshal lingered behind. Clem couldn't help but think he was the most fortunate man in all of Bandera to have the job he had and to have friends like Slim.

Roy Clinton

CHAPTER 9

The first thing I need to do is to stop Summerall and Carmichael," I said to Howard.

"How will you do that?"

"I need to prepare an injunction to stop them from dismantling Great National. Would you mind if I sit at your desk?"

"Of course not, John. Please make yourself at home." Howard dropped his head and added, "I guess that sounded strange. This has been your home longer than it's been mine."

"But it's your home now," I added as I settled into the familiar chair and surveyed the vast desk. "Howard, I need some paper and a pen. May I open the drawers to get what I need?"

"Certainly. I still keep paper in the top right drawer, right where your father kept it."

For the next several minutes, I wrote trying to remember the legal language I learned in law school. There were multiple strikeouts so I knew I'd need to rewrite it once I got the language correct.

"What'll you say in the injunction?" asked Howard.

"I'll give proof of my ownership of Great National and then ask the court to stop Summerall and Carmichael from taking any actions concerning the company. I will further demand the previous actions they have taken be reversed."

"Fortunately, they haven't yet broken up the company," Howard said. "About the only thing they've done is to take over the headquarters building and fire most of the senior staff. I guess that's the thing that hurt me most. We're more like family in the office. Most of the employees were long tenured. It will be good to tell them they still have jobs."

"You should be able to get word to them by tomorrow. Howard, I've made a mess of this document but I think I have all of the proper language in place. Now all I need to do is to recopy it."

"Would you mind if I make a suggestion?" asked Howard.

"Of course not."

"A few months ago I bought a Sholes and Glidden Type-Writer. I can make your injunction look like it was printed to be included in a book."

"I've read about that machine but I've never seen one. I know my father had a couple of other printing machines several years ago but he was never really satisfied with them." I watched Howard move to the back corner of the office and pull a drape off a boxy machine.

"E. Remington and Sons just started manufacturing these. In

fact, I bought one of the first ones sold in New York," Howard explained as he lifted the machine and moved it over to the desk. "If you don't mind, I'll be able to prepare that document for you in a few minutes."

I watched as Howard placed paper in the machine and deliberately struck the keyboard with his index fingers. He carefully removed the paper from the machine and turned to present it to me. In less time than it would have taken me to rewrite the injunction, Howard had produced a professional looking document.

"Thank you, Howard. Now if I can use your buggy, I'll get this over to the federal courthouse."

"Why are you filing in federal court? Great National's a New York company."

"It is but our railroad tracks go from state to state. The only way to stop Summerall and Carmichael is to use the federal court."

"That makes sense," said Howard. "Certainly, you may use the buggy. Do you mind if I come with you?"

"I'd like that very much," I said. We both moved toward the door and put on our coats and hats. It had been snowing earlier in the day but the sky was now clear and the temperature was still very cold.

We arrived at the courthouse about twenty minutes later and filed the injunction. It wouldn't take long for Summerall and Carmichael to learn instead of owning Great National, they were merely stockholders. They did own a significant portion of the company but they were nowhere near having controlling interest. As best as I could tell, they owned about fifteen percent of the stock. I was determined to see what I could do to make them want to sell. While they couldn't harm the company any longer, I didn't want them to have any association with the company my father had built.

A few days later, I was with Howard at the mansion when Alvelda told us there were two very angry men who wanted to speak with us. They refused to give their names but told Alvelda she better get Howard and me or she would be sorry.

"Alvelda, have the guards bring the men in," I said. "We have a good idea who they are." She politely closed the door and alerted the Pinkerton guards on her way to the front door.

Two officious men with heavy mustaches barged into the office. I stood to greet them. Both men refused to acknowledge my outstretched hand. "Let me guess," I said. "You must be Summerall and Carmichael." Come in gentlemen and have a seat. To what do we owe the pleasure?"

The men stood motionless for a few moments and then started speaking at the same time. "You're gonna be sorry you butted in where you don't belong," said the sandy haired man.

"And you're gonna have to answer to the shareholders at the next meeting," the darker haired man snarled.

"I'm afraid you gentlemen have been misinformed," I said. "As far as the stockholders go, I own seventy percent of the shares in Great National and I've just made an offer to some investors to purchase an additional fifteen percent. You gentlemen do not own more than fifteen percent of the stock. While that is a sizable portion of the company, you aren't even close to having controlling interest. Your plan to dismantle what my father built is over. You can hold on to your stock if you'd like or you can sell it back to me. But what I can tell you is you'll not have a say in anything the company does and you will never get a chance to significantly increase your stake in Great National."

Both men doubled up their fists and continued to glare at me. They looked like they were mad enough to get physically violent but I didn't have to worry about them. The Pinkerton guards that flanked them moved closer to each man.

"Now gentlemen before you go," I said, "I would like to make you a one time offer. And I stress this offer will not be repeated and it is good only until the close of business tomorrow. I will purchase the stock you hold in Great National Railroad at fifteen percent above its value. At the end of the day tomorrow, if I have not heard from you, I will rescind the offer. Good day, gentlemen."

The guards took each man by the elbow and escorted them to the front door where Alvelda stood with their coats and hats in her hands. As they started to prepare for the cold, Alvelda opened the door and said, "I hope you gentlemen have a good day." They exited the house and the guards once again went to their places guarding the front and back doors.

Roy Clinton

CHAPTER 10

When I got back to my room at the hotel, it was dark but I knew I would not be able to sleep any time soon. The meeting with the President was still very much on my mind. My carefully guarded secret identity was now known, at least to a few. But I believed the President to be a man of his word and didn't think he would divulge my secret to anyone.

I sat down and began to put my thoughts on paper. First, I knew I had to get more information about the financial panic that had swept the city. I wanted to know more about Jay Cooke & Company. It was still not clear to me how Summerall and Carmichael got such a large block of stock in Great National. Then I needed to put an end to the speculation around the railroads, but I was not sure how I was going to do that.

As I wrote, the silence was broken by the sounds of fire engines. There were bells and sirens piercing the night air. Looking out my window, I counted as multiple engines passed below. As much as I wanted to find out what was going on, I knew the last thing needed was another nosey onlooker getting in the way of the professionals who were responding to the emergency.

It wasn't long before I could hear more sirens and bells indicating other fire engines were on their way. I knew there must be a large fire nearby. But my focus needed to be on trying to put the pieces together and coming up with a plan to try to keep the financial panic in New York from consuming the nation.

I closed my window and shut the drapes, trying to block out the noise. As much as I tried to concentrate on the financial problems of the city and the President's visit, I found it difficult to tune out the cacophony on the streets below. In the bathroom, I took some toilet paper and started to roll two small balls to insert into my ears when I heard a knock at the door followed by a voice.

"Housekeeping. May I turn down your bed, sir?"

I unbolted and opened the door.

An aging woman in a grey uniform said, "I'm from housekeeping. Would you like for me to turn down your bed?"

"Yes, please do so. And ma'am, do you know the reason for all of the sirens and bells?"

"No sir. I heard a large building caught fire but I also heard someone say it might not be an office building at all but a large house."

Immediately my thoughts went to Howard and the threats made against him. The mansion he lived in was only about a mile from the hotel. I ran from the room and headed to the elevator.

"Did I say something wrong, sir? I'm sorry if I did, sir. Would you like for me to continue turning back your bed, sir?"

I could hear the housekeeper behind me but I didn't stop to answer. All that mattered now was getting to the house where I was raised and making sure everyone was safe. After a few seconds waiting on the elevator, I gave up and took the stairs. My suite was on the top floor but I felt I had to get over to the mansion as soon as I could. I descended the stairs two at a time and made short work of the six flights.

In the lobby I ran to the desk and inquired about hiring a buggy.

"Yes sir, we have a buggy waiting just out front of the hotel."

I ran outside and jumped into the buggy. As I was getting in, I saw the sky was glowing red in the direction of my childhood home.

"Where to, sir?" asked the driver.

"Take me to the fire and don't waste any time."

"Well sir, I don't think it is wise to do so. I'm afraid we might get in the way of the firefighters."

"Please! I need you to drive me there immediately! I think that's my home burning!"

"Yes sir!" The driver cracked the buggy whip on the rump of horse. The buggy lurched forward and the driver yelled commands to the horse. In just a couple of minutes, we arrived at a barrier that had been placed across the road.

I jumped from the buggy and ran toward the barricade.

"Hold it, mister," said a uniformed policeman. "You can't go in there. This area is for emergency personnel only."

"But officer," I protested, "I feel certain that's my house burning."

"Go ahead, sir," said the policeman. "But stay out of the way. Don't get in the way of the firemen."

I raced up the street being careful not to trip on the jumble of fire hoses that littered the street. When I got to the fire scene, I could see a smoldering pile of rubble that had once been the regal mansion built by my father. Howard Hastings was sitting on the curb with his head in his hands. His face was covered in soot and dark rivers of tears were pouring down his cheeks.

I sat down beside him and put an arm around his shoulder.

"I'm sorry, John," said Howard. "There's nothing I could do. I woke up and smelled smoke but didn't know where it was coming from. When I finally realized the house was on fire, I ran down to the rooms the staff occupy and tried to get them all out." He wiped his tears with his sleeve and continued. "John, I'm afraid Alvelda's—I'm afraid...."

I listened as he struggled to get the words out and started fearing the worst.

"John, Alvelda's been hurt. She's hurt bad. The firemen just brought her out. I thought she was out of the house. She must have gotten trapped inside. By the time the firemen brought her out, she was burned badly. They took her to the hospital. I just watched them drive her away. John, what are we going to do?"

"What hospital did they take her to?" I asked as Howard

continued to weep and cradle his head in his hands.

"I think they took her to Bellevue but I don't know for certain."

"Howard, I'm going to see her. I can't be any help here but I want to see Alvelda."

"You go ahead, John. I hope you get there in time." Howard wailed for a moment and then continued to cry softly.

I hugged Howard and ran back to my hired buggy. "Take me to Bellevue Hospital just as fast as you can."

"Yes sir," said the driver as he once again shouted for his horse to run hard. The crack of his whip punctuated each command.

We were only about four blocks from the hospital. The driver got there and stopped near the ambulance entrance. I jumped from the still moving buggy and entered the hospital and ran to the nurse's station.

"An ambulance just brought in a burn victim. Can you tell me where she is?" I implored.

"She has been taken back to a room to be treated by the doctors," said the nurse. "But you can't go back there."

I was already running down the hall as the nurse called after me.

"Sir, you can't go back there," said the nurse but I continued to run. I could see a room that had several nurses entering and exiting. I got to the door and looked in to see Alvelda lying on the bed. Her clothes were gone and a sheet covered her torso leaving her limbs exposed. I could see the burned flesh on her arms and legs, she was crying and the medical personnel were trying to comfort her. The smell in the room was nauseating. I realized I smelled her life-threatening burns.

"Alvelda!" I shouted as I entered the room.

"You can't come in here," shouted a nurse as she tried to block my path. "We have to take care of her now. There may be time for visitors later."

A doctor called out to the nurse. "Let him in. I don't think she can last much longer. I'm sorry, sir. We're doing all we can but her burns are very serious."

I looked at Alvelda and realized the worst burns were those on her arms and hands. She had some burns on her head and her legs were blistered. The only part of her body I could see that didn't look burned was the top of her head that was covered by her thick hair.

I moved closer to her and reached up and gently touched her head. "Alvelda, can you hear me? It's John."

She opened her eyes and said, "Johnny! My Johnny boy. I'm so glad you came to see me. Johnny, I think I'm hurt bad. Make 'em take good care of me, Johnny. I don't want to die."

"You're not going to die Alvelda. I'll make sure you get the best care available," I said as I rubbed her head.

"I'm so scared, Johnny, and I hurt so bad. Get them to make me stop hurting."

"That's enough, sir," said the doctor, "She needs to rest as we tend to her. If you will wait outside, I'll come out and tell you of her progress."

"I'll be right outside, Alvelda," I said as I leaned down to kiss the top of her head. "You're gonna be fine. Just wait and see."

Outside I walked back toward the ambulance entrance and found a small waiting room. I asked a nurse on duty there to please tell the doctor who was treating Alvelda where I was so he could give me a progress report.

There was a pot of coffee on a small stove. I helped myself to cup after cup as I waited to hear some word from the doctor. After a couple of hours waiting, the doctor came into the waiting room. His face looked drained so I feared the worst. I stood and walked over to the doctor.

"Doctor, is she...is she..."

"She's still alive," said the doctor. "But she is very critical. Most patients who have been burned so badly just don't survive. Her body has received the greatest trauma imaginable. And she's losing fluid because of her burns. Often it's the fluid loss that proves fatal."

"There has to be something you can do, doctor," I said. "Who is the best doctor you know of?" I grabbed the doctor by the shoulders and looked intently into his eyes. "Whoever it is, I want you to send for him immediately. Something has to be done to save Alvelda."

"Take it easy, sir," said the doctor and he tried to remove my hands from his body. I held tight. "We're doing all we know how to do. But I think you need to prepare yourself just in case."

I was stunned. Slowly, I released my hold on the doctor and sunk into a chair. How is it possible that Alvelda could die? She had always been there for me. When I was a little boy, Alvelda was the one I could always go to whenever I was afraid. She would know just the right words to comfort me.

"Sir, I didn't catch your name though I did hear the lady call you Johnny."

"I'm John Crudder," I said.

"Ah yes. I thought I saw a resemblance to Robert Crudder. He was no doubt your father. I'm Dr. Thomas Maxwell."

"That's right. Did you know him, Dr. Maxwell?"

"Not personally but I had seen him at the hospital many times."

"Really? I don't recall my father ever being ill," I said trying to make sense of what the doctor told me.

"Oh, he wasn't a patient. Your father was a major benefactor of the hospital. In fact, the wing we're in was donated by your father. I'm certainly happy to meet you, though I wish it was under different circumstances."

"Really! I didn't see his name anywhere. I have to assume that was by design."

"Yes it was, John. I didn't know who your father was for a number of months after I first saw him here," said the doctor. "Some of the time he would be with the hospital administrator but at other times he was by himself just walking around and observing. I finally asked the administrator who he was. After all, I'm the Chief of Medicine here and I thought I had a right to know the identity of the man. The administrator took me to his office and said the man I saw was Robert Crudder and he was trying to figure out how he could best help the hospital. Then he told me he knew a very large contribution would be made to the hospital but under no circumstances was I to reveal the source of the gift."

"Thank you, Dr. Maxwell. I didn't realize my father made donations to the hospital, though I'm not surprised. He was always looking to make a difference in the world and, as I have found out, he did a lot very quietly, behind the scenes."

"Your father was a great man. I thought all the more of him when I saw his desire to help others but was not seeking recognition for himself."

"Thanks again, doctor. I want to get back to Alvelda. Who is the best physician you know of? I don't mean to depreciate your skills but there has to be someone who knows more about treating burns than other doctors. If we could get the best doctor here to treat her, who would you get?"

"I'm not offended at all, Mr. Crudder. Actually, the answer to your question is an easy one. Dr. Samuel Gross of Philadelphia. He's a professor at the Jefferson Medical College. I've trained with him and I think he's the best physician in the country— especially when it comes to burn care. In fact, Dr. Gross developed the treatment we're using with Miss Alvelda. During the war, Dr. Gross saw many soldiers die from burns, mostly due to the loss of body fluids. He developed a treatment where he would mix paint—like what an artist would use—with linseed oil. He mixed it to the consistency of heavy cream and then applied it so it completely covered the burns. Then he would apply a cloth dressing to keep the ointment in place. Just a few minutes ago, we completed that treatment with Miss Alvelda. All we can do right now is wait to see if she recovers."

"What would it take to get Dr. Gross to come here? Could you contact him and ask him to come?" I asked. I was desperate enough that I would have done anything in my power to help the lady who was probably more of a mother to me than my own mom.

"I'll be glad to send him a telegram right now," said the doctor. "He's been a friend and mentor for many years. I'll do all I can to convince him to come and help."

"Thank you, Dr. Maxwell. Don't let me keep you. Please send the telegram as soon as you can and then get back to helping Alvelda."

"I'll dictate it to my nurse and then get back to our patient."

Dr. Maxwell stood and shook my hand and hurriedly walked away. Though I knew nothing had changed over the past few minutes, I did have a sense of hopefulness for the first time since I got to the hospital. I looked down the hall and could see the doctor giving instructions to a nurse. She was carefully transcribing what the doctor was dictating.

Within the hour, I saw Dr. Maxwell walking hastily down the hall. I stood immediately thinking he was bringing me bad news about Alvelda.

"What is it, doctor? Is she...." I couldn't bring myself to finish the sentence.

"No, Mr. Crudder. Miss Alvelda is actually resting now for the first time. We have been able to ease her pain enough so she could sleep. I contacted Dr. Gross and told him of our patient. He approved of our treatment so far and said it would be safe to increase the dosage of morphine. As soon as we did that, Miss Alvelda dropped into a deep sleep."

"That's good news, doctor. Did you ask Dr. Gross to come here to help?"

"I did indeed. He's on his way to the train station right now and should be arriving here by late afternoon. I'll have a buggy waiting at Grand Central Depot to bring him here just as he arrives."

"Thank you, Dr. Maxwell," I said as I simultaneously shook his hand and let go of a river of tears. "I'm sorry for such a display of emotion, doctor. I'm not used to feeling like my hands are tied. Usually I can find a solution to a problem and move on. But with this, I just don't know what to do."

"Actually, Mr. Crudder, you did find a solution that I hope works well. When you asked me about the best doctor to treat Alvelda, I immediately thought of Dr. Gross. But I would not have thought of consulting him or of asking him to come here were it not for you."

I continued to weep as I thought about how much Alvelda meant to me. Dr. Maxwell pulled me into a soft embrace and held me tightly. I returned the hug and sobbed on his shoulder. I silently prayed that God would let Alvelda live. After a few minutes I released the doctor and returned to my seat in the waiting room.

Roy Clinton

CHAPTER 11

About a week after the meeting of the Bandera Cattleman's Association, Marshal Williams had gathered more information about which ranches were missing cattle and how many. He found Slim in his office and went over carrying two cups of coffee.

"Hello Marshal," said Slim. "I see you didn't come to drink my coffee. Thanks for bringin' me a cup. Has your coffee makin' improved?"

"You tell me, Slim," said the marshal as he handed over the cup. Slim took a sip and grinned. He looked at the marshal and shook his head.

"Clem, I must say your coffee is as good as I've ever had. I'd be pleased to drink it anytime."

"Thanks, Mayor. Word's gotten out that I make pretty good coffee now. I even have people stoppin' by just to sit and chew the fat. They never did that before. Only thing they ever did was to come by and tell me their business and leave. I want you to know I do like having people enjoy comin' by just to talk and drink coffee. And I owe that to you. Thanks, Slim!"

"You're welcome, Marshal. Now, as much as I'm enjoyin' your coffee, I have a feelin' you have somethin' else on your mind."

"You're right, Slim. I've gathered the figures from the ranchers and if my arithmetic is correct, about one hundred and fifty head have gone missin' over the past three months. And from what the ranchers are tellin' me, there may be more missin' but they just haven't had time to track their losses. I think I ought to call another meetin' of the Cattleman's Association. What do you think?"

"Hold on a bit, Marshal. It probably is a good idea to have another meetin' and I know Barlow said you could call a meetin' any time you liked, but I think it might be wiser to ride out to Barlow and tell him what you've found out. If there needs to be a meetin' called, let him do it. In the end, the result is the same. The meetin' will take place but it will have been Barlow's idea. Don't you think he would like that better?"

"You're right, Slim. They were awfully nice to me in the last meetin' but it does make more sense to have Barlow call the meetin' himself if he thinks it's necessary."

"There's more need for another meetin' than you realize. I'm sad to say I've lost some more cattle, at least twenty more head," said Slim.

"When did it happen?" asked the marshal.

"I'm not sure. They may've been gone for some time. I went

down toward the southern end of the ranch to check on the herd that stays in the pastureland around a little lake just north of Hondo. I routinely count the cattle when I move to another part of the ranch. There're twenty head gone and maybe more."

"Why'd they risk taking so many at once," asked Clem, "especially when they've been careful to only take a few at a time?"

"Well, they probably know we don't always have hands on that end of the ranch. It was easy for 'em to get away with that many head without getting caught."

"What do you think they've done with 'em?"

"Marshal, if I had to guess, I think they just drove them over to San Anton. It's only about forty miles. They could sell 'em without havin' a lot of questions."

"Any idea who might have taken 'em?"

"No. There haven't been any strangers around other than a few new hands I've hired over the past several months. And I don't suspect any of them. They all seem to work hard and get along well with the other hands."

Slim struggled with the thought that there were once again rustlers operating in Bandera. He shuddered as the memories of Charlotte's kidnapping and knowing how close he came to losing her, the H&F, and his own life. Whatever it took, he was determined not to let history repeat itself.

Roy Clinton

CHAPTER 12

Shortly after sunrise, Howard came to the hospital. When I saw him, I stood and we both hugged and cried. Howard smelled of smoke and his clothes were covered in soot. I told him what I knew about Alvelda's condition and the treatment Dr. Maxwell was using with her. I also told him about Dr. Gross and how he was on a train headed for New York.

It was comforting to have Howard with me. I felt a sense of hopefulness with Dr. Maxwell and knowing Dr. Gross would soon be here to help. For the first time, I believed Alvelda would survive her burns. We spoke of Alvelda for a while and before long the conversation centered on the fire.

"Howard," I said as I turned to face him, "please tell me what happened."

"I don't really know. As I told you, I smelled smoke. At first I thought it was coming from outside the house. I wasn't really concerned. But then I noticed some wisps of smoke coming from underneath my bedroom door. When I opened the door, smoke poured in. The hall was hot and I could see flames leaping out from another door. Fortunately the stairs were behind me, away from the fire. I got my wife and children out and then I ran down to the second floor and saw that it, too, was on fire. When I got to the first floor, I thought I would find that the fire had started in the kitchen but there was no fire at all in there. I'm still not sure where the fire started but when I went into the wing containing the service workers' rooms I saw it was also on fire. John, that just didn't make sense to me. Those rooms are a long way from the fire I saw in the other part of the house. It was like two separate fires that started at the same time.

"Anyway, I started banging on the doors of the employees. I thought I got all of them out but I realized later that the fire was burning right at Alvelda's room. In fact with the flames covering her door, I didn't even realize that was her bedroom. John, if Alvelda dies it will be because of me."

"That's nonsense, Howard. You didn't cause the fire and you didn't harm Alvelda. But we're going to find out who did, and Howard, whoever did this, will pay with their lives. Do you have any idea who would burn down the mansion?"

"I've been thinking about that and all I can come up with is Summerall and Carmichael. I don't think they did it themselves but I'll bet they hired someone to do it."

"That sounds right to me, Howard. When we know for certain Alvelda will pull through, I'm gonna make it my job to find out who did this and see they're brought to justice—one way or another."

Roy Clinton

CHAPTER 13

Late in the afternoon, Dr. Maxwell came into the
waiting room followed by an older man who was
tall and had a handsome face. He was bald on top
but had long flowing white hair.

"Mr. Crudder," said Dr. Maxwell, "this is Dr. Samuel Gross.
Dr. Gross, may I present Mr. John Crudder."

"I'm honored to meet you, Doctor," I said as I enthusiastically
shook his hand. "Thank you so much for coming."

"I'm glad to do so, Mr. Crudder. When Dr. Maxwell told me
of the situation and asked me to come to New York, I hesitated
only for a moment. I was thinking about my teaching
responsibilities and of the young doctors studying under me. But
then I thought they could take care of things in the clinic while I
was gone. Besides I've been working on improving my treatment
protocols and thought this would be a good place to try them
out."

"I am so very grateful you've come to help. I'll forever be in your debt." I cleared my throat and continued. "Gentlemen, may I present Mr. Howard Hastings, the CEO of Great National Railroad. Howard, I'm pleased to introduce Dr. Samuel Gross."

"And I'm pleased to meet you," Dr. Gross said. "From what I gather from Dr. Maxwell, it was your house that burned resulting in Miss Alvelda's injuries."

"That's right, Doctor," said Howard. "And the fire didn't start by itself. John and I will find those responsible and see that they're brought to justice."

"Well, that's your work," said Dr. Gross. "My work is waiting at the end of the hall. If you will excuse me, gentlemen."

As he walked down the hall, Dr. Maxwell turned to Howard and then to me.

"I'm not sure quite how to say this, gentlemen, but would you please consider getting away from the hospital long enough to clean up? Frankly, this end of the hospital smells of the fire that destroyed your home. For the sake of other patients, I appeal to your sense of civility and ask that you have a good bath and a change of clothes. Miss Alvelda is receiving the very best of care. You can get away for an hour or so to clean up."

"You're right, Doctor," I said. "I have been so concerned about Alvelda that I hadn't even noticed how our presence was impacting the rest of the hospital. Howard, let's go clean up."

We shook Dr. Maxwell's hand and walked out of the hospital.

CHAPTER 14

Order. Order!" shouted Barlow over the loud talking. "Please come to order. This meetin' of the Bandera Cattleman's Association will commence." Gradually the men settled down and took their seats but they continued to talk as Barlow pounded a gavel on the table. "We all know why we're here. The cattle thieves have continued operatin' and seem to be steppin' up their stealin'. The marshal came to visit me and told me several of you have complained of losin' more cattle. So I want to hear from the marshal now."

Clem Williams slowly stood and walked to the front of the room. "Thank you, Mr. Barlow. I don't reckon there's much I can add except it seems 'bout everyone I've run into over the past few weeks has said they were missin' cattle. Some, just a few head but others were missin' more. Slim told me he's missin' about twenty more head."

"That's right, Marshal," said Slim. "I went down to the south end of my ranch near Hondo last week. I always count cattle when I ride through. As best I can tell, I'm missin' twenty head from that part of the ranch. But I was already out about ten head—maybe more."

"Any idea who might have taken 'em," asked Barlow.

"No I don't. But it seems way too familiar. When the Tarpley bunch was operatin', I was losin' a steady stream of cattle. If I wasn't sure we wiped out their operation, I'd think they were still in business."

"How can you be sure there aren't still some of them around?" asked Barlow.

"If you had asked me that a couple of months ago, I would've said there's no chance," said Slim. "One by one the rustlers were caught or killed. And we didn't have any cattle losses for a couple of years. But now it seems like it's started up again."

There was a loud murmur among the cattlemen as they all talked at once. Then Red stood and shouted above the others, "I think what we need is better leadership in the Cattleman's Association. Barlow, if you were doin' your job, this wouldn't have happened. And as far as that goes, I think the marshal is also responsible. Marshal, you're responsible to protect our property and it don't seem like you're doin' what you were hired to do."

"Now just wait a minute, Red," said Slim. "It's easy to point fingers and assign blame. But you can't expect the marshal or Barlow to be everywhere at once. They're not the cause of your problems."

"Well, I know someone else who is responsible. And that's you, Mayor. Slim, I recall you bein' mighty upset with the old mayor and council for the way they were runnin' things. We thought it would be different when we elected you but it seems you're just as crooked as they were."

Slim charged toward Red and drew back his fist but Barlow stepped in and grabbed Slim's arm before he could deliver the punch.

"Red, I've had about enough of your accusin'," said Slim. "We've got enough trouble without you recklessly throwin' accusations around. If you've got somethin' else to say, you better make sure it's helpful. If it's just more of you tryin' to stir things up, you better think twice before you speak."

Red sat down and looked visibly shaken. It's not that Slim was much bigger or stronger than Red. But Red saw something in Slim's eyes that told him he had pushed him as far as he could get by with.

"All right," shouted Barlow. "Let's everyone settle down. And Red, I agree with Slim. If you've got somethin' helpful to say, then say it. Otherwise, you best keep quiet." Barlow straightened his vest and took a deep breath as he walked back to the front of the room. "Does anyone have any suggestions as to what we do now?"

"Well, Mr. Barlow," said the marshal. "I think everyone needs to keep their eyes open for strangers and keep watch on their cattle. 'Til we get this rustlin' stopped, it would be helpful if anyone missin' more cattle would report it to Barlow, Slim, or me. We can keep checking with each other to make sure we've got a good picture of what's goin' on."

Barlow nodded and said, "Marshal, that's a fine idea. So men, even if you are only missin' one or two head, make sure you report it so we can keep accurate count of how many head are missin'. And if you discover you thought you had some cattle missin' but find they just wandered off, be sure to let us know that as well. We need to have a precise count of what rustlers are takin'."

Slim stood and faced the men. "Have any of you hired anyone lately who is not from around here?"

"You mean like strangers?" asked Red. "I've got a couple of new hands but they're good men that I can vouch for."

"Yeah, Slim," said Barlow. "I've hired some new hands over the past couple of months but I've also been watchin' 'em pretty closely. I don't think they're involved in anything."

"We've added some men on the H&F as well," added Slim. "My point is that cattle are bein' taken. And they're either bein' taken by strangers or by someone we know. I'd like to think some of our new hires are the most likely suspects. Just keep your eyes open. And if you see anything that seems out of line, don't take any action. Just report it to the marshal or Barlow. And if you see me in town, you can report it to me. But I can tell you, I'm not gonna be spendin' much time in town 'til we catch the thieves. I'll be on my ranch keepin' watch over my herd. And I suggest you men do the same."

"Unless anyone else has anything they want to say, I think we can adjourn," said Barlow. "I'll get word to you if I think we need to have another meetin'. Now let's get back to watchin' our cattle. But if anyone wants a beer before you head back, meet me downstairs. I'm buyin'."

Barlow banged the gavel and the men began filing out of the room and down the stairs and were soon standing elbow to elbow in the Cheer Up. Mugs were filled and the conversation about the cattle thefts continued.

"Slim, I thought you were gonna hurt Red," said Barlow. "Normally, I would think Red could take care of himself but you had a crazy look in your eye."

"I don't know what came over me," said Slim. "One minute I was calm and listenin' to the conversation. And the next I was in a blind rage and determined to beat Red senseless. I guess Red just reminded me of how out-of-control Bandera was with the old council. Plus, I never wanted to be mayor. You know that. The only reason I agreed to it was to try to help stabilize things in town. But when Red popped off and started accusin' me of not doin' my job, I'd just heard enough. Barlow, thanks for steppin' in and keepin' me from doin' somethin' I know I'd later regret."

"You're welcome, Slim. I knew that wasn't like you. But I have to tell you, I was pretty angry at Red myself. He'd just accused me of not doin' my job. I was thinkin' about hittin' him myself when you started toward him."

Slim smiled, "That would have been a sight—you and me both jumpin' Red. And don't forget, he'd also accused the marshal of not doin' his job. It's a wonder all three of us didn't give him a good beatin'." Slim took another swallow and banged his mug back down on the bar. "Thanks for the beer, Barlow. I've got to get back to the ranch."

"You're welcome, Slim. I've got to get goin' myself."

Over the next few minutes the rest of the cattlemen finished their beers and left the Cheer Up. As the men mounted up, most spurred their horses, wasting no time as they returned to keep watch over their cattle. Losing even three or four head represented a significant loss even to the larger ranches. But for smaller ranches, the loss of a single head was financially devastating.

Slim returned to the ranch and found Owen in the barn. He filled him in on what took place in the Cattleman's Association meeting. When he was through talking, Owen had questions of his own.

"So, Slim, do you think it's possible some of our new hands are responsible for the cattle we've lost?"

"I don't know what to think. All I'm sure of is we're missin' too many head to think they just wandered off. I was about ready to think they'd just gotten lost and would turn up later. But when I went to the Hondo end of the ranch last week and realized that part of the herd was short by at least twenty head, I knew someone had taken 'em. Owen, I think we need to let some of the men who've been with us the longest in on what's happenin'. They can help us be on the lookout for anything that doesn't look right. There's no way the two of us can keep watch on the whole ranch or every hand."

"That's a good idea. Can I tell 'em we know some cattle thieves are operatin' around here?"

"Sure, Owen. Tell 'em to keep the information to themselves but to suspect anyone and everyone that looks suspicious. And let 'em know we have to watch the new hands. Someone is takin' our beef. We've got to put a stop to it now."

Roy Clinton

CHAPTER 15

The doctors told us Alvelda was out of danger. She would probably be in the hospital for several weeks and most likely require skin grafts to help her heal. With her health on the mend, it was time for me to find out what was behind the financial panic that had gripped New York.

I set up a series of meetings with each of the CEOs of the major railroads. It didn't take me long to get a picture of what had been happening. Each of them told of rumors they had heard and about pressure being brought on them to either sell out or change the way they did business. None of them had much information about where the pressure was coming from but it seemed to be highly coordinated and was relentless. Some of the companies, in order to survive, had broken their businesses up into smaller companies so they could sell off the unprofitable parts and continue to survive. Several of them told of sabotage to other companies and of the fear the same would happen to them.

The last meeting I had was with the president of Northern Pacific Railroad. They had begun construction on a transcontinental railroad about three years earlier. When Jay Cooke & Company gave financial backing the next year, the company gained great momentum.

My buggy arrived at the office of Northern Pacific and I immediately went to the president's office. A secretary was sitting at a desk outside of his office and greeted me as soon as I arrived.

"May I help you, sir?" she asked in a very businesslike voice.

"Yes ma'am. I would like visit with Mr. Cass, if he's in."

"I'm sorry, sir, but while he is in, he is very busy. Did you have an appointment?"

"No, I do not. If you would please tell him that John Crudder would like to see him. I will not take much of his time but it's urgent I speak to him today."

"I will see, sir. But I don't think he will be able to see you. His schedule is full today."

She stood and walked to the door of the president's office, knocked lightly and then let herself in. A few seconds later the door opened and a large man with a long curly white beard walked out.

"Mr. Crudder. Please come in. I'm George Washington Cass." He walked toward me and stuck out his hand. I shook it as he continued talking. "I was a friend of your father's for many years. He and I have had many dealings—all of them good, I must say. But please forgive me. I want to convey my condolences for your loss. Robert was a great man."

"Thank you, Mr. Cass. And thank you for seeing me without an appointment."

"Think nothing of it. And please call me George."

"All right, George. Please call me John."

"To what do I owe the honor of your visit, John?"

"Well sir, I'm trying to make sense of what's been going on in the railroad industry over the past few years."

"I'm trying to do that myself," said Cass. "I suppose you heard what happened with Jay Cooke & Company."

"I did, but only a few days ago. I sold a portion of Great National some years ago and settled down in Texas. I left Howard Hastings in charge and most people including Howard thought I had sold the entire company."

"John, that's a nice surprise. I too thought you had sold the company. I'm glad to hear you still own it. Your father was one of my closest friends so I'm glad to know it is still in the family. You say you live in Texas. What brings you to New York?"

"It's a long story but the heart of it is that some stockholders were attempting to take over Great National. They thought they owned controlling interest and had Howard thrown out of his office and made plans to dismantle the company and sell off the rolling stock and then the tracks."

"Who would do such a thing? I can't believe anyone would want to break up Great National."

"While there were several people involved, the two main conspirators are William Summerall and Buckminster

Carmichael."

"I should have known Summerall and Carmichael were mixed up with Cooke & Company. In fact, I think it was those two who got the company to buy up several railroads. The company got overextended and was forced to suspend operations. Jay Cooke himself was forced into bankruptcy but I think Summerall and Carmichael were the two men who were primarily responsible for his downfall."

"I didn't know that," I said. "Where did they get their wealth? I haven't been able to find out much about them."

"They have been involved in one shady deal after another. All the while they have a façade of respectability about them. They sit on the stock exchange and appear to be upstanding businessmen. But I know for a fact that they've been involved in deals that have left people not only homeless but also penniless."

"What kind of deals are you talking about?" I asked.

"Well, while they were encouraging Cooke to buy other railroads, they bought up smaller railroads themselves, most of them outside of New York. It seems that they just happen to come along after a company experiences a great setback. One company lost all of the stock in its main warehouse when a water main broke and flooded the building. Another lost their headquarters to a fire. And there was another where the president and vice president were convicted of fraud. Summerall and Carmichael just happened to swoop in and buy the company for pennies on the dollar. So far, I don't think any charges have been made because there's just not enough evidence to convict them.

All those crises were concocted and played out because of them."

"I knew I didn't have any use for them but I had no idea they were involved in activities like you just mentioned." I contemplated what Cass had told me and wondered if there was a way for me to appeal to the greed of the two men and perhaps to put them out of business. Over the next half hour, I listened to Cass talk about the methods Summerall and Carmichael used to force companies into selling.

"George, thank you for your time and for some very enlightening conversation." I stood and extended my hand. "I'll let you get back to your day. Your secretary told me you were particularly busy today."

"That's quite all right, John. Things are always busy around here. I was glad to get a break. Please come see me again. And convey my regards to Howard."

As my buggy pulled away from the office building, I knew I needed to bring President Grant up-to-date on what I found out. I went to the hotel and found Howard and his family had moved in there until they could line up other living arrangements. Howard was in his suite and let me in when I rang the bell.

"Howard, I need to go to Washington to give a report to President Grant. Would you like to go with me?"

"Certainly I would. When are you going?"

"I want to send a telegram first to let him know we're coming. But I want to leave as soon as possible. Would you see if there's a train leaving today for Washington while I go send the telegram?

"I'd be glad to," said Howard as we both headed out the door to catch the elevator to the first floor. Howard went to the front desk and I went down the street to the Western Union office. Hurriedly I wrote out a message and addressed it to the President's assistant, knowing he would pass it on to the President.

Jeffrey Jameson
Washington, D.C.

Have found information you need to know. Will arrive in D.C. tomorrow or the next day.

John Crudder
New York City

When I got back to the hotel, Howard met me in the lobby and told me there was a train leaving for Washington in just over an hour. We went upstairs and packed for our trip. The train was scheduled to arrive in Washington just over a day after leaving New York. I packed three suits and hurried to the lobby. When Howard arrived, we took a buggy to Grand Central Depot. We barely got our luggage on board when the conductor called out.

"All passengers going to Washington, the train is about to depart. All aboard."

Howard had arranged for us to have a Pullman car so we would be able to sleep more comfortably. As soon as we settled into our seats and the train lurched forward, our journey began. I nodded off before the train was up to speed. When I woke up it was nearly dusk. It was then that I realized just how much sleep I had lost over the past few days as I sat at the hospital concerned about Alvelda's health. I pulled down the window shades, folded out my sleeping berth, and lay down. The next thing I knew it was morning.

I dressed and made my way to the next car to find Howard drinking coffee and reading a newspaper. I got myself a cup and took a seat beside him. We purchased sweet rolls for our breakfast and contemplated our meeting with the President. I had never been to Washington before and was looking forward to the experience.

Roy Clinton

CHAPTER 16

Slim and Owen continued watching the ranch carefully. Owen had identified ten hands he thought could help keep a more careful watch on the ranch. The hands were assigned to stay on various parts of the ranch and to challenge anyone who didn't have business there. On the third day of patrolling the H&F, Owen saw three riders he didn't know head south across the ranch and then pull up at the Medina River to give their horses a drink. Owen took his horse through the trees along the river. He drew his six-gun and called out as he came out of the cover.

"All right you men. I don't know what you're doin' here but you've got no call to be on this ranch. Oh, Mr. Nichols. I didn't know that was you."

"Hello, Owen. You can just call me Red, like everyone else in town. No need to get all riled up. We were just cuttin' through the ranch on our way to San Anton."

"You gave me quite a start, Mr.—er—Red. When I saw the

three of you, I thought I had caught our rustlers."

The men with Red laughed and Red joined in. "Yeah, I guess we look like desperate criminals all right."

"Well I'm sorry I pulled a gun on you," said Owen. "We're just lookin' out for anything that's out of place or anyone who doesn't seem to belong."

"That's all right, Owen. We're doin' the same thing on our ranch. Well, I guess we need to be goin' if we're gonna make San Anton before dark."

Red touched the brim of his hat in a salute to Owen and reined his horse across the river. The two strangers with him followed and Owen watched and wondered why he had never seen the other men around Bandera.

At suppertime, Owen made his way to the dining hall and walked over to Slim's table.

"Howdy, Owen. What've you got on your mind? Aren't you goin' to get some food?"

Owen sat down and said, "I will in a minute. Guess who I saw on the ranch today?" Slim stopped eating and stared at Owen.

"Who?"

"Well, I was headin' over to check to see if any of our cattle had wandered over beyond the Medina," said Owen. "Remember, we moved them all back on this side of the river so we could keep closer watch on them."

"I remember, Owen. Are you gonna tell me who you saw or not?"

"Sorry. I saw Red Nichols and two riders with him I haven't

seen before."

"What were they doin'?" asked Slim.

"They were just waterin' their horses. I couldn't see who they were so I slipped up to the river and pulled my gun on 'em. I was sure I'd caught our rustlers. I hadn't seen Red yet but knew the other two men were not from around here."

"What happened?" asked Slim.

"Well, Red called out to me. At first I kept my gun leveled at the whole bunch. The other two men looked mighty tough. If Red hadn't been with them I'd have been sure they were rustlers. But Red acted all calm like. He said they're just headed over to San Anton and were cuttin' through the ranch."

"That sounds right," said Slim. "We have a lot of people cut through the ranch. No harm done."

"I know you're right, Slim. But if you could've seen the men and the way their eyes kept cuttin' back to Red as he spoke. Somethin' was off. I don't know how to explain it. But somethin' just seemed out of place."

Slim dropped his head as he thought about what Owen had said. He forked a piece of steak and started chewing as he continued to contemplate.

"Thanks for lettin' me know, Owen. Maybe it's nothin' to worry about. But then again, who knows. In the mornin' I'll go see Barlow and the marshal and tell 'em what you saw. Keep a good eye out and let me know if you see anyone else that doesn't belong.

The next morning Slim rode into town and reined up at the

marshal's office.

"Hey Marshal. Do you have any coffee that's fit to drink?" said Slim as he swung the door open.

"Howdy Slim." Marshal Williams smiled and said, "You know, I've been told the coffee here is might as good as you can find anywhere in town." Slim walked to the stove and poured himself a cup.

Carefully Slim put the cup to his lips and blew gently on the hot liquid. Then he took a swallow and said, "Marshal, I think you have gotten the hang of it. This is some good coffee."

Williams continued to smile and refilled his own cup. "So Slim, what're you doin' in town so early. Don't tell me you just came to drink my coffee."

"No, Marshal. I wanted to tell you and Barlow somethin' that happened on the ranch yesterday. Owen saw three men cuttin' across the ranch. He rode up behind them and got the drop on 'em. As he was sizin' up the men, he realized Red Nichols was with them. Red said they were just ridin' through the ranch on their way to San Anton. Owen put his gun away but said the two men with Red looked like they were up to somethin'. He said he hadn't seen them around here before."

The marshal had a startled look on his face. "What's wrong, Marshal?" asked Slim.

"Barlow was in here the day before yesterday and told me about the same thing. He said he was ridin' on his ranch and saw three men cut across it. When he rode up closer to 'em, he realized it was Red and two of his hands. He didn't think too much of it since Red's ranch is not that far from his. But he said he didn't like the look of the men with Red. He said he had never seen 'em before and if Red hadn't been with 'em he would've been sure he'd caught his rustlers."

"Marshal, I'm headin' out to see Barlow. You want to ride with me?"

"I shor do. Somethin' ain't right around here. We've got to find out what it is."

The marshal and Slim took the road north out of town. They rode about five miles when they got to Barlow's ranch. The spread was impressive, and the ranch house was made of stone that had been quarried nearby. As they approached the house, Barlow walked out onto his front porch with a rifle and brought it up to challenge the riders.

"Howdy, Marshal. Howdy, Slim," said Barlow as he dropped the rifle. "I'm not used to havin' company this time of mornin'. Sorry for the cold reception. I thought you might have been up to no good. Come on in and have some coffee. I just put on a fresh pot."

"I think I've had enough coffee for the day," said Slim. "Thanks just the same."

"So what's so important both of you would come to see me?"

"Barlow, I had some visitors on my ranch and I wasn't so concerned about 'em 'til the marshal told me you've had the same visitors."

Slim and the marshal swung down and tied their horses to the hitching rail.

"Yesterday," Slim said, "Owen found Red and two of his new hands on my ranch. I didn't think it was unusual. They said they were just on their way to San Anton and were just savin' time by cuttin' across my ranch. I told the marshal about it and he said you have had the same visitors on your ranch."

Barlow was startled by what he was told. "That's 'bout the story they told me. When I found 'em, Red said they were just ridin' across my ranch lookin' for some of their cattle that were missin'. He said they thought they might have wandered over to my spread. But now that I think about it, that don't make sense. His ranch is nearly two miles from where I found him. Cattle don't wander that far without help."

"Do you think Red could be behind the rustlin' that's been goin' on?" asked the marshal.

"Well, I do know Red has been quick to point an accusin' finger at everyone other than himself," said Barlow. "And I also know Red believes he hasn't gotten a fair shake in town. He's struggled in the past to make it on his spread. He hasn't had that many cattle until the past couple of years."

Slim picked up on Barlow's comment. "Now that you say that, I've noticed Red has seemed to be more prosperous lately. And he seems to have had a marked increase in the size of his herd. The only reason I know that is Owen told me Red recruited two of our hands to come work for him. Red told 'em his operation was growin' and he could pay 'em higher wages than we pay on the H&F."

For the next hour, Slim, Barlow, and the marshal examined the possibility that Red was their rustler. They didn't like the idea of even suspecting someone who was their neighbor. Red had been in Bandera most of his life. And, except for him accusing others of not tending their jobs, he was a respected citizen. But as they compared the two recent sightings of Red and his two hands, there was just too much similarity in the occurrences for them to ignore.

"I hope we're wrong about thinkin' Red could be involved in the rustlin'," said Barlow.

"So do I," said Slim. "But we need to face the fact that somethin's just not right. Red and his hands could've been doin' just what they said. Or they could've been up to no good. I think it's time for us to find out what's true."

"What do you have in mind, Slim?" asked the marshal.

"I think we ought to set a trap and see if we catch any rustlers," said Slim.

"How do you suppose we do that?" asked Barlow.

"Barlow, Red's ranch is only a couple of miles from yours," said Slim. "What if you let it slip that you had to go to Austin for a few days and that you hoped the rustlers wouldn't bother your cattle while you're gone."

"I could do that," said Barlow. "There's a box canyon on the end of my ranch that has a nice pasture that hasn't been grazed in the past month. I could let it be known I'm gonna move my herd there for them to graze while I'm gone. With it bein' Friday, I'll bet Red will come into the Cheer Up this evenin'. I'll let my plans slip out and say I'm gonna be out of town for the next week."

"And we'll lie in wait to see if someone comes for your cattle?" asked Marshal Williams.

"Yes," said Slim. "But we need to find a way to get them to strike on a particular night. We can't stake out the ranch all week."

"That's easy. We're in the process of raising another barn. I'll just let it slip that on Tuesday of next week, I'm most concerned about my cattle because I'll have all of the hands involved in the barn raisin'. If Red and his bunch are involved, I don't think they'll be able to resist a herd of cattle unguarded that they can get to during the day time."

"That's great, Barlow," said Slim. "Let's meet at the canyon Monday evening. We can camp there and be on guard by first light. If Red is behind the rustlin', I'll bet they show their hand that mornin'."

That evening, Barlow was at the Cheer Up when Red walked in. When Red saw him, he went over to where Barlow was standing.

"Can I buy you another beer, Barlow?" said Red. "Just to show you I don't have any hard feelin's about our meetin' the other day."

"Sure, Red. I didn't take offence to what you said. I know you and all the other cattlemen are frustrated knowin' someone is stealin' our beef. You were just speakin' your mind."

"Glad you see it that way. With us bein' neighbors and all, we need to stick together."

"You're right about that," said Barlow. "We have to watch out for one another. What I know is I can't be everywhere I need to be watchin' for rustlers. I have to carry on with business. In fact, I'm gonna be gone all next week. On Tuesday, the men are all gonna be raisin' a new barn for me. So on Monday, they'll move the herd into the box canyon at the end of my ranch. The cattle will have plenty of grass to eat there and I won't need the hands to watch after them."

Red's eyes sparkled as he heard the news. *What a perfect set up*, he thought. *I'll be able to help myself to as many of his herd as I want.*

"So you're gonna be out-of-town next week," said Red. "Where ya headed?"

"Just to Austin. I've got some business that can't wait. Otherwise I wouldn't miss the barn raisin'. I sort of feel bad knowin' the men will be doin' all of the work without me. But the good news is the barn should be finished when I get back home. We've got all of the lumber out at the ranch. It'll take the hands all day and maybe the next to finish the barn but I know they'll get it done."

"Well, have a safe trip," said Red. "And again, Barlow, no hard feelin's?"

"No hard feelin's. Thanks for the beer," said Barlow as he drained his mug and headed out the door. He headed down to the marshal's office and saw a lamp burning through the window. He walked in and found Clem sweeping out the cells.

"Hello Marshal. Well, it's all done. I saw Red and told him the cattle will be waiting and unguarded on Tuesday. Please let Slim know. I'm headed back to my place now and will lie low until Monday evenin'. Then I look forward to seein' you both out at the box canyon."

"I shor will, Barlow. I'll tell Slim and we'll see you Monday evenin'."

✳✳✳

Monday, right at dusk, Slim and the marshal headed out to the canyon at the end of Barlow's ranch. They made their way to the canyon and had their horses slowly ascend a bluff near the back of the canyon. When they got to the top, Barlow greeted them and told them he had supper ready.

"Thanks for comin' men. I hope you came hungry. I had my cook make us some fried chicken and a nice peach pie. I think the pie may still be hot."

"That sounds mighty good to me," said the marshal. "I get tired of eatin' my own cookin'."

"What do you mean, your own cookin'?" asked Slim. "You know you eat most meals at the Better Days and their food is fine."

"Well, Slim, what I meant to say is if I was cookin', I would rather have somethin' someone else cooked for me 'cause I know it'd be better. That's all I was sayin'."

Barlow and Slim both laughed as they listened to the marshal awkwardly try to explain himself.

"I agree with you, Marshal," said Slim. "I would rather eat someone else's cookin' than I would my own." The men finished their meal and bedded down for the night.

✱✱✱

About an hour before dawn, Slim gently woke both men. "We better get up and get ready. Sorry there won't be any coffee. We can't risk someone seeing our campfire. I suggest that we take our places around the canyon and wait. I have a feelin' we're gonna have company real soon."

"I have that same feelin'," said Barlow.

The three men split up and worked their way around the canyon so they each had a good view of the pasture below and the cows that were peacefully grazing. Shortly before first light, three riders rode into the pasture. They continued riding and came up near where Barlow had been hiding. As Barlow watched, Red directed the men with him to cut out twenty head. Barlow stood up and called out to the riders.

"Red, I thought you were behind the stealin'," said Barlow. "I can't say as I'm surprised seein' you here." Barlow raised his rifle to the riders. Red pulled his six-gun and shot Barlow. As he did, the other two riders pulled their guns and also shot Barlow.

Slim and the marshal raised up from their hiding places and shot toward the riders, though they were too far away to see who they were. The men quickly swung down and slapped their horses on their rumps. As they did, the cattle spooked. The men returned fire and ran for cover. The cattle stampeded and for a few moments, it was impossible to tell where the rustlers were. Slim finally got a clear view and shot one of them.

The marshal worked his way down the bluff and found Red hiding behind a bush. "You better come out of there with your hands in the air," said the marshal.

Red stood up and dropped his gun. Slim made his way to where they were standing as he held the gun on Red.

"Where are the rest of your men?" asked Slim. "It seems like they left you here alone. Marshal, go check on Barlow."

"I'm already there," said the marshal. "He's dead. Looks like he was shot three or four times. Red, I think you're gonna be facin' murder charges." Slim looked for the other men and found them. "Slim, these two are dead. Looks like one was shot in the shoulder but both of them were trampled by the cattle. I think it's kind of fittin' the cattle they tried to steal ended their lives."

CHAPTER 17

We arrived in Washington a little after noon and hired a buggy to take us to the Executive Mansion. Since this was my first opportunity to visit the nation's capital, I asked the buggy driver to take us by the Washington Monument and the United States Capitol. I was spellbound by the beauty of the monuments. I made up my mind that this would not be my last time in the city.

A few minutes later we arrived at the Executive Mansion. I'm not sure what I was expecting but was surprised to find that the President's home was not that much larger than the home my father built. We arrived and knocked on the door. A butler opened the door, greeted us, and allowed us to be seated while he inquired as to whether the President would see us.

I was struck by the beautiful paneling in the parlor room where we were sitting. Large portraits lined the walls. Some of the paintings were of former Presidents. I assumed the women in the photos were their wives. A marble fireplace was in the center of one wall and a massive chandelier hung from the ceiling. It looked like it had room for two dozen candles or more. I thought about how difficult it would be to light them in the evening. After a few minutes, the door at the other end of the room opened and President Grant walked in with a cigar between his lips.

"Gentlemen. I'm sorry to keep you waiting." The President walked to us and extended his hand. "Please come in. I was just getting ready to eat. Could I interest you in joining me?"

"It would be our pleasure, Mr. President," said Howard. I was glad he responded. Other than the last several days in New York, it had been a long time since I had been invited to dinner in a more formal setting.

We followed the President into his office and then out the other side into a small dining room. From the opulence of the sitting room we were in, I was expecting the President's office to be regal. I was surprised to find it was quite Spartan in appearance. There was a desk that was smaller than the one that had been in Howard's home office and a rather plain looking desk chair. Two utilitarian sofas were pushed against the walls. They were well worn and didn't seem appropriate for the room. Although a small chandelier hung from the ceiling and a lovely fireplace graced one wall, the rest of the office revealed bare walls and no decoration of any kind. On the President's desk was a single photo of a woman; I suppose it was Mrs. Grant.

As we entered the dining room, again I was shocked at the furniture. The table was worn and stained and surrounded by several mismatched ladder-back chairs.

"Come have a seat anywhere you like," said the President. "We don't stand on formalities around here."

Howard and I took a seat as the butler entered the room and began filling water glasses. President Grant had yet to take the cigar from his lips. His continual puffing soon filled the small room with smoke. When our meal arrived, the President laid his cigar in an ashtray that was beside his plate.

"I know this is not as fancy as what you're used to." The President paused to cough. "After spending so much time in the Army, I'm actually most comfortable living in a tent. This dining room reminds me of those days. This is the same table I used in the field. My senior officers and I planned battle strategy around this table. We also had our meals on it and in the evenings the officers would join me for a nightcap or two.

"But I'm sure you didn't come here to discuss my office furniture. What's on your mind, John?"

"Well, sir," I said to the President. "I've found out some information that sheds light on how the financial crisis developed. But the bad news is that there may not be much that can be done in the near term to mitigate the damage that's already happened."

Grant's cigar continued to smolder in the ashtray as the butler brought in several platters of food. I paused as the food was set on the table. There was a platter of what appeared to be barbequed ribs, one of mashed potatoes, one of carrots, and another of green beans.

"During the war, I got introduced to barbequed pork ribs. I'd never heard of such until I made a tour of the South," said the President. "When I came back to the North, I tried to find someone who knew what they were and how to cook them. Finally, I found a former slave who not only knew how to cook them but her ribs were even better than what I had in the South. She is now my cook so I get to have ribs every week if I want them. She just calls her creations 'down home cooking' but it is the best I've had."

Howard and I nodded in approval as we dug into food.

"Now, John, you were telling me what you found."

"Well, Mr. President, it seems two men, William Summerall and Buckminster Carmichael, are responsible for most of it. They were buying up smaller railroads outside of New York, some of which were in Minnesota. They evidently convinced Jay Cooke to buy up additional railroads and rights-of-way, with the thought of being able to then complete what was to be the second transcontinental railroad. Cooke aggressively sold bonds in Northern Pacific Railroad to finance the new venture. The purchases of the new smaller railroads were so aggressive that the company had begun depending heavily on the money from new bond investors to pay for the new land and railroad deals. Finally, Jay Cooke & Company was so overextended, they couldn't pay their obligations. They didn't have enough reserves to continue operation. The company collapsed and Jay Cooke himself was forced into personal bankruptcy.

"Mr. President, the most alarming thing is the methods

Summerall and Carmichael used to get the companies to sell. In one case, they forced freight companies doing business with a railroad to stop shipping on that railroad. A series of unexplained instances of sabotage and theft in the shipping companies forced them to find other means of transport. As a result, that railroad had to sell before they were forced to shut down."

President Grant lit another cigar as his previous cigar continued to smolder. "What else, John?"

"In another case, a railroad had several of its trains derail. They were never able to determine the cause but they knew the causes were manmade. One such incident could be explained. But when they kept happening, they knew someone was out to ruin them. They too were forced to sell."

"So was Cooke & Company involved?" asked the President.

"They were involved in that they bought some of the railroads." I laid down my fork and wiped my face with the cotton napkin and I had a feeling I wouldn't be eating any more. "However," I continued, "there's no evidence they knew about the things that happened to make the railroad companies want to sell out. I think Summerall and Carmichael were behind all of the underhanded things that happened. Jay Cooke's contribution was that he wanted to acquire the railroads and he bought more than his company could assimilate."

The cloud of smoke in that small room was lowering over the table. I thought any moment we would be fully engulfed. Just then, the butler appeared and walked to the window. He opened it just a few inches and then opened the transoms above the two doors to the room. Thankfully, the smoke began to dissipate.

"Keep going, John. What else do you know?" asked the President.

"There was another case where a company had mysterious fires that destroyed three freight warehouses. After that, the same company had several new locomotives explode, killing the engineers and firemen."

"Explode! What would cause them to explode?"

"It seems in each case, the boilers on the engines became so over pressured they simply exploded. The official cause was the use of faulty pressure regulators. But for that to happen repeatedly to the same company makes it clear sabotage was involved. The company did a good job of keeping reporters from connecting the incidents and then quietly sold out to Jay Cooke & Company."

President Grant sat back and took several puffs on his cigar. "I don't see how this many things could be happening and someone not notice or be able to put the pieces together and realize something underhanded was going on."

"I'm afraid there is more to tell. Summerall and Carmichael bought up a large block of stock in Great National Railroad. Thinking they had control, this is when they forced Howard out and said he was fired. When they found out they didn't own the company, Howard's home mysteriously burned down. When you were visiting with us in New York, you met Alvelda, who has always been an indispensable part of the household."

"Yes, I recall meeting her. I especially remember the little sandwiches she made. They were the most delicious I've ever had."

"Well, Mr. President, Alvelda was burned badly in the fire. She is in Bellevue Hospital in critical condition."

"That's horrible, John. Do you think she will survive?"

"We hope so, sir. That is our prayer. A specialist that deals with burns has been brought in to care for her. Howard and I will get back to New York and do what we can to make sure she gets the best of care."

"People who would do such a thing should not be allowed to walk the earth," said President Grant. "I think there must be a special place in hell for those responsible."

"I agree sir."

"What needs to be done, John?"

"As I said earlier, the damage to the economy has already been done." I paused as I thought about what to say next. "Unfortunately, Mr. President, I don't see anything that can be done to lessen the financial impact on the nation. In fact, I'm not going to be surprised if this has a significant impact on European markets."

"I think you're right about that, John. The first financial ripples are already crossing Europe. I fear we may be in store for a global depression."

"I hope that is not the case, Mr. President. So rather than being able to quickly fix the financial crisis, I think the focus should be on keeping those responsible from causing any more financial havoc."

"I agree completely. What did you have in mind, John?"

"Well, sir, as best as I can tell, no one has witnessed any of the sabotage. There's not enough evidence to convict Summerall and Carmichael. They occupy seats on the New York Stock Exchange and are pretty well insulated from suspicion."

"Do you think we'll ever have enough evidence to bring those responsible to justice?"

"Perhaps, Mr. President. I just don't know. What I do know is, as of now, there is not even enough evidence to charge them with a specific crime. My fear is what they will do in the meanwhile."

"We cannot allow these men to inflict any more damage to our nation's economy," said President Grant. "People have been killed and companies have been wrecked. Now it appears our nation—perhaps the whole world—will continue to suffer financial woes due to their shenanigans. Mr. Crudder, I must ask you to contact your friend Midnight Marauder and ask him to intervene on behalf of the nation. Will you do that, sir?"

"Yes, I will contact him, sir. What are your orders for him?" I asked. If I was going to take care of this problem on behalf of the President, I wanted to know exactly what he expected of me.

"Tell him to find the men responsible for causing this financial crisis. From this point forward, I commission him as a special agent to the President of the United States. He is to track down the men responsible for this financial catastrophe. He must then eliminate them to keep them from continuing their financial mischief. And the sooner he does so, the better it will be for the country. Mr. Crudder, do you think our friend can solve this problem before the end of the year?"

"I don't know, Mr. President. But I do know he'll try his best."

"That's good enough for me," said the President as he exhaled a large cloud of smoke across the table. He pushed back from his chair and stood. Immediately, Howard and I stood. It was obvious the meeting was over. He walked around the table and slapped me on the back as he led us back through his office to the front door of the Executive Mansion.

"Howard. John. It has been a pleasure to have you in my home. I know you have work to do so I will not keep you from it. Please let me know when your mission is complete." He had walked us briskly to the front door and out onto the colonnade. "Good day, gentlemen," said the President as he closed the door. Howard and I stood there for a minute and thought about what had just transpired and the abrupt end to the meeting.

"John," said Howard, "it seems the President has been very clear about what he expects of you. What are you going to do?"

"The only thing I can do is to follow his orders. Let's get back to New York so I can get started."

Roy Clinton

CHAPTER 18

Clem Williams took his prisoner to jail and then went to the telegraph office to send a message to the district judge in San Antonio with a request for a trial to be set as soon as possible. In about two hours the judge replied and said he could be in town in two weeks to conduct the trial. The marshal rode over to Slim's office to give him the word.

"I was hopin' you would be in town," said Williams. "You saved me a trip out to your ranch. I just got word from the judge in San Anton that he will be here Monday after next to conduct the trial."

"That's good," said Slim. "The sooner the better. I'm still a bit surprised Red was behind the rustlin'. But I guess we'll never know what makes a man turn to crime."

"Slim, I was just figurin' about Red. Do you reckon he needed more money or was he just greedy?"

"I don't know, Marshal. I can't figure out some people. Maybe he was jealous of Barlow for havin' such a large spread. I'm not sure what was behind it but I'm glad we caught him in the act. I don't think there is any way he'll be able to get away with his stealin', no matter what story he tries to tell."

"What do you think the judge will do with him?" asked the marshal.

"Well Clem, they always used to hang cattle thieves. But over the last few years, I've seen most of 'em sent to the penitentiary in Huntsville. But since he killed Barlow and was responsible for the death of his two hands, I won't be surprised if the judge calls for him to be hanged."

"Slim, there hasn't been a hangin' since I've been marshal. I don't know how I'll feel havin' to watch someone be killed like that."

"Marshal, remember you watched Red kill Barlow and you know he was responsible for the death of the other two men."

"I know," said the marshal. "I just never figured on havin' to be part of a hangin' party."

"We'll deal with that when the time comes. For now, Clem, the only thing you need to think of is keepin' your prisoner secure until the trial."

✳✳✳

The judge came into town Sunday evening before the trial was to take place. Word had already gotten out about the upcoming trial. Shortly after the sun was up the following morning, the town was already filled with farmers and ranchers who rode into town to witness the trial of someone they had known well. Some of them had known Red all of their lives.

The judge entered the courthouse followed by the marshal. Many of the spectator seats were already filled. The judge rapped his gavel on the bench.

"How many of you men want to be on the jury this mornin'?" No one in the courtroom raised a hand. "That's fine. Marshal, I want you to go out on the street and round up all of the men you see and tell them to meet me in the courtroom."

In a few minutes the marshal was back and the remaining seats in the courtroom were filled.

"I want each man here to come up here and sign in or make your mark on this piece of paper," said the judge. "Since I don't have any volunteers for jury service, I'm gonna appoint some of you to serve. And I don't want any excuses as to why you can't serve."

After all had registered, the judge looked at the list and said, "I'm gonna call out every third name on the list. When your name is called, come on up and have a seat in the jury box."

One by one the judge called out the names. On two occasions, he asked whose mark was on the paper by calling out the names before and after the mark and asking the identity of the man standing with them in line. With the jury complete, he turned to the marshal and instructed him to go get the prisoner.

Slim was seated on the front row of the courtroom, knowing

he and the marshal would have to give testimony as to what they witnessed. When Red was brought in, he was seated at a table with his attorney. The attorney had long flowing white hair and wore a smartly tailored suit. He had on a heavily starched white shirt and a tie that had a large gold slide.

"The court will come to order," shouted the judge as he banged his gavel on the bench. "Marshal, will you please read the charges. The defendant will stand as the charges are read."

"Yes sir, Judge," replied Marshal Williams. "Randolph Nichols, better known as Red Nichols, is charged with cattle rustlin' and the murder of Jedidiah Barlow, and contributin' to the deaths of two men I've never met."

"How does the defendant plea?" asked the Judge.

"I'm not guilty, Judge," said Red.

"Marshal, put your hand on the Good Book and swear to tell the truth."

"I swear I'll tell the truth, Judge."

"All right, Marshal. State your full name and then tell the court what happened."

"I'm Marshal Clem Williams. Well, Judge; me, and Slim Hanson suspected Red was the one behind the rustlin'...."

"I've got to stop you there. Marshal, you just tell what you did," said the judge. "Mr. Hanson can give his own testimony about what he suspected when you're through."

"I'm sorry, Judge. It started on Monday, two weeks ago. Slim and I met Barlow at the back of his ranch. We planned to camp out that night so we could keep watch over the cattle. We figured cattle thieves were gonna make a play for 'em the next mornin'."

"Why did you believe that?" asked the judge.

"Because Barlow let it be known he was gonna be out of town that whole week and that his entire herd would be in the box canyon at the end of his ranch. He told the men in the Cheer Up that all of his hands moved the herd so they would be free to raise a new barn on Tuesday."

"What happened next, Marshal?" asked the judge.

"Like I was sayin', me and Slim met Barlow Monday evening and camped out so we could be in place if the cattle thieves came the next mornin'."

"Keep goin', Marshal. What happened next?"

"We was awake and watchin' before first light. That's when we saw Red and his two men ride up into the middle of the herd. Red told the men to cut out twenty head and they commenced to cuttin' 'em out when Barlow called out to Red so he would know he had been caught. That's when Red shot Barlow."

"I object, your honor," said the attorney sitting with Red.

"Don't you be objectin' in my courtroom. That ain't the way I do things," said the judge. "I know that's the way law schools are teachin' you young lawyers now. But in my courtroom, you don't interrupt. You listen until it's your turn. Then you'll have time to ask questions. 'Til then, you just sit quietly. Now, Marshal, continue with your testimony."

"Well, like I was sayin', that's when Red shot Barlow. The men with Red started shootin' too. Slim and me returned fire. That's when the cattle got spooked and knocked the two riders to the ground. They got trampled pretty bad by the cattle. One of the men had a bullet in his shoulder but that weren't what killed him. They both died from bein' trampled by the herd."

"And what happened to Mr. Nichols?" asked the judge.

"Well, somehow he slipped off his horse and hid out. When he saw me and Slim had him dead-to-rights, he gave up. I arrested him and put him in jail. That's when I telegraphed you, judge."

"Anything else you would like to add, Marshal?"

"Just one thing, Judge. I saw Red shoot Barlow. It was the most cold-blooded thing I ever saw."

"Now it's time to ask your questions, Mr. Attorney," said the judge.

"Thank you, your honor. I'm Hezekiah Mumford for the defense. Marshal, you said you heard Mr. Nichols give an order to cut out twenty head."

"That's right," said the marshal.

"Isn't it true that what Mr. Nichols actually said was he had counted twenty head that he knew were from his own herd and he told the men to cut them out?"

"No," said the marshal. "He didn't say anything of the sort. He just told his men to cut out twenty head."

"But you don't know that he intended to steal them, do you?" asked the attorney. "Mr. Nichols never said, 'I want you men to steal twenty head of Mr. Barlow's cattle,' isn't that right?"

"No, he didn't say that. But when the three of them slipped into the herd at first light, they weren't makin' a social call. They were there to steal cattle."

"Let's move on, Marshal. You said this happened at first light. So in other words it was still pretty dark. Isn't it true you didn't actually see Mr. Nichols fire his gun but it was one of the two men with him?"

"No, that's not true," said the marshal. "I could clearly see Red pull his gun and shoot Barlow. Red did it. I saw it. You can't make me believe it was any other way."

"I have no further questions, your honor."

"You may step down, Marshal," said the judge. "Mr. Hanson come up here, put your hand on the Good Book, and swear to tell the truth."

Slim walked to the judge holding his hat in his hands. He put his hand on the Bible and said, "I swear I'll tell the truth, Judge."

"State your full name and then be seated."

"My name is Richard Hanson but folks 'round here just call me Slim."

"All right, Mr. Hanson, now you tell what happened."

"Well, Judge, it was like the marshal said. I did suspect Red was in on the rustlin'. I caught Red and the same two men on my ranch...."

"I object your honor," said the attorney as he jumped to his feet. "Mr. Hanson..."

The judge banged his gavel. "Now son, I'm not gonna warn you again. I told you there's not gonna be any objectin' in my courtroom. You'll have time to say all you want to say later."

"But I have to object," said the attorney.

"And I have to find you in contempt of court. That'll be five dollars, son. You can pay up now. And if you interrupt again, it will be ten dollars more."

Having been duly chastened, the attorney stood and walked to the bench and laid down five silver dollars. He hung his head as he went back to his seat.

"Now, Mr. Hanson," said the judge, "you can continue with your testimony."

"Well, Judge, my ranch foreman caught Red and his two hands on my ranch. They were waterin' their horses when I came by."

"Hold it right there, Mr. Hanson. You mean, you didn't see them on your ranch?"

"That's right, Judge. But my foreman did and I saw them when they came to rustle Barlow's cattle."

"Well, I need to stop things right here. We'll need to hear from the ranch foreman. What's his name?"

"His name is Owen—uh—it's Owen—uh—Judge. I know I know his last name. He's been with me more than 15 years. But I just can't think of it right now. We don't go much by last names on the ranch...."

"Simms," shouted someone in the back of the courtroom. "It's Owen Simms. I'm here, Judge. I can tell you what I saw if you want to hear it."

"Certainly, sir. Mr. Hanson, you may step down for a few minutes. Mr. Simms, come up here and place your hand on the Good Book and swear to tell the truth."

Owen walked to the front as Slim stepped aside. They smiled

at each other as Slim took his seat and Owen approached the witness chair.

"All right, Mr. Simms. Place your hand on the Good Book and swear."

Owen did as directed and put his hand on the Bible and said, "I swear, Judge."

"All right, Mr. Simms, tell us what you saw."

"Well, Judge. It's just like Slim here said. I saw three men on the H&F. They weren't any of our hands. I know 'em all. They were waterin' their horses on the Medina River. I thought they might be rustlers. I snuck up on 'em and got the drop. I pulled my six-gun and told 'em to reach. Then I saw it was Red here," he motioned his head toward Nichols. "So I thought I knew they weren't rustlers and I lowered my gun. Red said they were just cuttin' through the ranch on their way to San Anton. That sounded right. We have lots of folks do that—I mean cut through the ranch on their way to San Anton."

"Keep going, Mr. Simms."

"Well, I was listenin' to Red and I started lookin' at the two men with him. Judge, there was just somethin' not right about 'em. You know what I mean? They were just all shifty eyed and lookin' at Red and lookin' at me. That's when I knew somethin' wasn't just accordin' to Hoyle. You get my meanin'?"

"I follow you, Mr. Simms. So what happened then?"

"Well Judge, I told Slim what I saw. I guess that's it, Judge. I don't know nothin' else."

"Thank you, Mr. Simms. I'm just glad you were in the

courtroom today."

"I wouldn't have missed it, Judge. I want to see these rustlers pay for what they've done."

There was a loud murmur in the gallery.

"Order! Order!" shouted the judge as he rapped his gavel loudly on the bench.

"All right, Mr. Hanson. Come on back up. Mr. Simms, you can go back to your seat. Mr. Hanson, you're still under oath. So take a seat and keep on telling us what happened."

"Well, your honor, as I was sayin', after Owen told me what he saw, I got with Barlow and Marshal Williams and told 'em what I knew. I found out Barlow had seen the same three men on his ranch and it just didn't seem right. Judge, I don't know rightly how to explain it but it just seemed Red suddenly had more cattle than he ever had. He even hired away two of my best hands promisin' to pay them more than they got on my ranch. Then the other thing that struck me as odd was the way Red kept accusin' others of not doin' their jobs and lettin' the rustlin' continue."

"Keep goin', Mr. Hanson," said the judge.

"Well, like the marshal was sayin', we were talkin' with Barlow and decided to set a trap to see if we could catch the rustlers. Barlow was in the Cheer Up when Red came in. Red bought him a beer and told him he didn't want any hard feelin's from Red criticizin' his leadership of the Cattlemen's Association. Barlow said he told Red he was gonna be out-of-town the next week and he was havin' his hands move his herd into the box canyon so they wouldn't need to be watched. That would allow his men to build the new barn. He'd been plannin' the new barn for some time so he thought this would be a good time to lay a trap for the rustlers.

"So the marshal and I rode out and met Barlow at the box canyon. Early the next mornin', Red and his men rode right into the middle of the cattle. We heard Red tell his men to cut out twenty head. That's when Barlow stood up and confronted Red. Red pulled his six-gun and shot Barlow dead. Then the marshal and I stood up to return fire and the other two men started firin' at us. The cattle started to stampede and both of the hands got thrown. The cattle trampled them but somehow Red just sort of disappeared. That's when the marshal caught him hidin' behind a bush and arrested him and took him to jail."

"Is there anything else you want to add, Mr. Hanson?" asked the judge.

"No, your honor. It's just as I said. Red and his two men were tryin' to steal Barlow's cattle and Red shot Barlow dead."

"Mr. Mumford, you may cross examine the witness," said the judge.

Mumford stood and straightened his vest and walked slowly to the witness stand. "Mr. Hanson. How long have you known Mr. Nichols?"

"I guess most of my life," replied Slim. "I don't remember him as a boy but I know he's been around Bandera at least thirty years."

"And in all of that time," said the attorney, "have you ever known Mr. Nichols to be involved in any illegal activity?"

"No, I don't reckon I have."

"Then how is it you came to suspect Mr. Nichols of being a cattle thief?"

"I felt it was not a coincidence that Red and his two men were found on my ranch and on Barlow's. And Red was quick to accuse others of not doin' their jobs. It was like he was tryin' to shift suspicion to others so he could hide his own actions."

"So your foreman just saw Mr. Nichols riding across your ranch. And when you heard about it, you yourself said you didn't think anything of it when he told your foreman he was simply cutting across your ranch to go to San Antonio."

"Yes, but then he did the same thing on Barlow's ranch. And he wasn't headed to San Anton then."

"Mr. Hanson, isn't it true that you were angry with Mr. Nichols because he had recruited, as you said, two of your top hands to work for him? Didn't you decide then you were going to frame Mr. Nichols for cattle rustling?"

"No, that's not true! Yes, Red hired two of my hands. But you have to understand, any cattleman will tell you hands drift from ranch to ranch. It's not unusual for men to be workin' for me one month and then go to another ranch the next. That's just the nature of the work."

"I have no other questions, your honor."

"Thank you, Mr. Hanson. You may step down," said the judge. "Now we will hear from the defendant. Mr. Nichols, come place your hand on the Good Book and swear to tell the truth."

Slowly, Red stood and walked to the judge and placed his hand on the Bible. "I swear I'll tell the truth, your honor."

"Please state your name and be seated."

"My name is Randolph Nichols but everyone just calls me Red."

"Mr. Mumford," said the judge, "you may come and question your client."

"Thank you, your honor," said Mumford. "Mr. Nichols, please tell the court what happened on the Tuesday morning in question."

"Well," said Red. "Like the other ranchers, I had been losin' cattle. I must have had thirty or forty head stolen. On that mornin', I took my men and we rode over to Barlow's ranch. Barlow told me he was puttin' all of his cattle in the box canyon on his ranch. I thought that would make it easy for me to look through his cattle and see if any of mine were mixed in his herd."

"Did you tell Mr. Barlow you planned to look through his cattle?" asked the attorney.

"No, I didn't. I thought if Mr. Barlow was the one doin' the rustlin', I didn't want to tip him off. I was figurin' on bein' able to look through all of his cattle without him bein' around. Especially since it was very early in the mornin'."

"And what did you find, Mr. Nichols?"

"I did see several of my cattle. At least it looked like they were my cattle. It was still pretty dark and I couldn't see the brands real good. But I told the men to cut those cattle out so I could move 'em away from the rest of the herd and let me take a closer look at 'em.'"

"What happened next, Mr. Nichols?"

"That's when Barlow stood up and started shootin'. He shot one of my men and I thought he was gonna shoot me. That's when I returned fire. I didn't even know it was Barlow. All I knew was someone was shootin' and I was about to be killed. I was just defendin' myself."

"Thank you, Mr. Nichols," said the attorney. "Your honor, I think we've proven Mr. Nichols is not a cattle thief, but he was actually on the trail of the real thief, Mr. Jed Barlow. And I think we have clearly shown that Mr. Nichols is not a murderer at all. Rather, he was exercising his God-given right to defend himself. It is regrettable that Mr. Barlow was killed. But he brought it on himself by cattle rustling and by taking a shot at my client.

"You men on the jury know my client. Many of you have known him for many years. He has never even been accused of doing anything that is illegal. He is a hardworking cattleman who has enjoyed the respect of the town. Mr. Nichols had every right to look for his missing cattle and to defend himself. Each of you men would have done the same thing in such circumstances. I ask you men to do what you know is the right thing and that is to find my client, and your friend, Red Nichols, not guilty of all charges."

"Gentlemen of the jury," said the judge. "Now it's time for you to render a verdict. You will all go into the jury room and decide if the defendant is guilty or not guilty to each of the three charges. He has been charged with cattle rustlin', murder, and contributing to the death of two men. This court will stand adjourned until the jury comes back with a verdict." The judge rapped his gavel once and stood up.

The noise level in the courtroom immediately rose as the spectators repeated various parts of the testimony. Some of those who had been seated left the courtroom and headed across the street to the Cheer Up. Slim and the marshal filed out and went over to the marshal's office.

"I could sure use a cup of coffee, Marshal," said Slim.

"Just let me add some wood to the stove and I'll have some coffee made in no time." They sat and waited while the coffee was being made. The marshal asked, "Do you think they're gonna find him guilty?"

"I don't know, Marshal," said Slim. "You never know with a jury. They're all good men but they have to weigh the stories they've heard. Red's attorney did a good job of givin' an alternate explanation of what happened. Only you, me, and Red know what really happened out there. Red was lyin' but the jury now has to decide who they believe. If they believe you and me, they'll find Red guilty. If they believe Red, they'll vote him to be not guilty."

"Slim, I never had to testify before. I have to admit I was nervous."

"You did just fine. The only thing anyone is expected to do is just to tell the truth. You did that. Regardless of what the jury decides, Clem, you did the right thing. You told just what happened. So you've done your duty."

Just then a shot was heard. The marshal and Slim ran into the street to see a man in front of the courthouse with his gun pointed toward the sky.

"The judge said that court will now resume. The jury has come back with their verdict," said the shooter.

The doors to the Cheer Up swung out as the saloon emptied out. Others who were strolling along the boardwalks hurried toward the courthouse. Slim and the marshal joined the flow of people and entered the courthouse. They walked to the front and had a seat just as the judge banged his gavel twice. The jury had been out less than half an hour.

"Let there be order in the court," said the judge. Then he turned toward the jury and continued. "Has the jury reached a verdict?"

The jury foreman stood and said, "We have, your honor. We the jury find the defendant, Randolph Nichols, guilty on all three charges."

There was loud talking as many of the spectators remarked about the verdict. The judge rapped his gavel twice more. "You will come to order," said the judge. Then he turned to address the defendant.

"The defendant will please rise." Slowly Red and his attorney stood and faced the judge.

"It is the judgment of this court," began the judge, "that the defendant is guilty of all charges and will be hanged by the neck until he is dead. Marshal, I instruct you to take the defendant back to jail and have a hanging scaffold built immediately. I will send for the executioner in San Antonio. The sentence is to take place at noon this coming Saturday. This court is adjourned."

Once again the noise level in the courtroom rose to the point where no single voice could be discerned. Some of the women cried. A couple of men shouted that they couldn't hang Red. He was their friend. Red slumped in his chair and began to cry. His lawyer tried to comfort him but Red was inconsolable. The marshal put handcuffs on Red and slowly walked him back to the jail. Slim walked with him and helped lock Red in his cell.

"I just can't believe it," said the marshal. "There's gonna be a hangin' in Bandera. I don't think there has been a hangin' here since those men were lynched in the war."

During the war, a Confederate patrol encountered eight well-dressed men from Williamson County. They were charged with "evading Confederate service" and taken into custody and were being transported to Camp Verde. It was suggested they be hanged for their crime. One by one, the men were lynched just south of Bandera while each man waited his turn. One of the men requested to be shot instead and his request was granted. However, the ramrod was left in the musket and when the man was shot, the ramrod pierced his body. After the war, all of the soldiers involved left Texas and none were ever found and brought to trial.

"Well, Marshal, the law has spoken. Red is guilty and he has been sentenced to hang. All we can do is see that the sentence is carried out. I'll help get men organized to build the scaffold."

Slim walked over to the Cheer Up and recruited six men to

build the scaffold. They would be paid out of the city treasury. The owner of the lumberyard was having a beer so Slim arranged with him to open up and supply the lumber needed for the hanging platform. Slim told him he would be by in the morning to pay him for the supplies.

By later that afternoon, the hanging scaffold was completed. Red had stood looking out his cell window watching the structure take shape. Throughout the construction, Red sobbed quietly and mumbled to himself.

The judge got back to Bandera on Friday evening to preside over the execution the next day. On Saturday morning, the executioner arrived from San Antonio. He introduced himself to the marshal and then proceeded to put his rope on the scaffold and check the trapdoor. He tied a sack of feed to the rope and repeatedly pulled the lever on the trapdoor. Each time the door swung open, the sack of feed would fall several feet and then be stopped by the rope. Red watched each time realizing he was seeing a rehearsal of his execution.

At noon, the judge made his way over to the jail.

"Well, Marshal," said the judge, "it's time. Get the prisoner and take him out to the scaffold."

Outside, the choir from the church had assembled and was singing hymns. The crowd gathered and men began coming out of the saloon to witness the first hanging many had ever seen.

Clem put handcuffs on Red and led him out of the jail. The marshal stopped as they got to the boardwalk. He was shocked to see the street full of spectators. Slim came over to Marshal

Williams and walked with him to the scaffold.

At the direction of the judge, the executioner took the prisoner up the scaffold and stood him over the trapdoor. The marshal and Slim stepped aside and watched as Red stood on the platform on the last day of his life.

"Do you have anything you would like to say before the sentence is carried out?" asked the judge.

"I just want to say, I'm sorry," said Red. "I never meant for anyone to get hurt. Everyone else had so many cattle. I didn't think anyone would miss one or two head. Then I got greedy and started takin' more. Before I knew it, my herd was growin' but I still wanted more. And I never meant for Barlow to get hurt. He had been a friend for many years. I'm sorry I shot him."

The executioner placed a black hood over Red's head and slipped the rope around his neck. He carefully placed the noose so it lay on Red's shoulder and a bit of slack draped down Red's back. When the executioner climbed down the stairs, he walked over to the lever for the trapdoor and looked toward the judge. The judge nodded his head once and the lever was pulled.

There was a collective gasp from the crowd as Red fell through the trapdoor. When he got to the end of his rope, Red's body came to a jolting stop. Just that quickly, justice was carried out and Red's life ended.

Roy Clinton

CHAPTER 19

Back in New York, I continued my investigation. Over the course of the next week, I interviewed other men who were involved in the railroad industry. I sent several telegrams to the former executives of the railroad companies that had been forced to sell. Each of them implicated Summerall and Carmichael in some way. But all of them denied having any specific evidence the two were behind the woes of their companies. It seemed they were long on suspicion and short on factual evidence.

I thought the best thing I could do was try to find out as much as I could about the two men. When I visited the New York Stock Exchange, I found they were highly regarded for their stock trading skills and were respected by their peers. Surreptitiously, I visited each of their brokerage offices. I didn't see either man. They were either cordoned off from the office workers in their private offices or they were simply not there. Both offices were models of efficiency. The employees seemed happy and content in their work.

Leaving the stock exchange, I went by the New York City Society Library to do some research on the two men. The library had an impressive collection of books and reference works. I found out the library was founded in 1754. In the late seventeen hundreds, the library actually functioned as the Library of Congress until the capital of the United States was moved to Washington DC.

With the vast resources at my disposal, it didn't take me long to read a great deal about Summerall and Carmichael. I was also able to find the addresses of their homes. Both of them appeared to own multiple residences but each owned only a single home in New York City.

Leaving the library, I had my driver take me by each of their homes. We didn't stop. All I wanted to do was to see where they lived. Their homes were both on Fifth Avenue, not far from where I grew up and where Howard lived until the fire. They were large, as were all of the homes in that part of town.

Back at my hotel, I started to put the pieces together. No less than a dozen of the current and former railroad executives I had contacted implicated Summerall and Carmichael in the problems of their companies. None had evidence but all had their own suspicions. Several also mentioned seeing two men in the vicinity of damaged property. The descriptions didn't fit Summerall and Carmichael but perhaps they were the ones who actually did the dirty deeds. One man was tall and slender and the other was much shorter but with a stocky build. I didn't get any other description but it was a safe assumption that these were the men Summerall and Carmichael had hired for their criminal activities. I guessed they were also the men who had burned down Howard's home and had hurt Alvelda.

Somehow I needed to find out who those two men were and learn as much as I could about what Summerall and Carmichael were planning to do next. The only thing I knew to do was to follow the men and see if they would lead me to another clue. I made arrangements to hire a buggy without a driver for the rest of my stay in New York. The hotel would see that it was hitched up each morning and care for the horse in the evening.

When morning dawned, I donned a nondescript suit and derby hat. I wanted to be able to blend in as easily as possible in the city without anyone taking too careful notice of me. Carmichael's house was the closest to the hotel so I went there first. I stopped the buggy a block down from the house with the buggy pointed in the direction of the stock exchange.

After waiting about fifteen minutes, a buggy pulled up in front of the house and Carmichael came out, said something to the driver, and entered the carriage. Instead of moving in the direction of the stock exchange, the driver turned the rig around and went in the opposite direction. After a few blocks, the driver turned left and stopped in front of a building that was surrounded by a wrought iron fence.

Carmichael climbed down and went to the gate and rang a bell. A formally dressed butler came out of the building and opened the gate to admit Carmichael. There was no name on the building but there were several other carriages nearby with drivers waiting and sitting in the front seat or, in some cases, waiting beside a buggy.

I was getting ready to investigate further when a buggy carrying Summerall arrived. The same butler responded to the ringing bell and admitted him through the gate. I guessed the building housed an exclusive club of some sort. Once Summerall was inside, I walked to the gate and rang the bell. The same butler responded and walked to the gate. Acting on my hunch I told the butler that I was interested in petitioning the club for membership.

"I'm sorry, sir, but one cannot simply apply to this club. One must be *proposed* for membership by a current member who is in good standing. Without a sponsor, one will find it impossible to acquire membership." I listened to the butler's proper English and studied his aloofness. He lifted his eyes a few inches above my head and turned to go.

"May I ask," I continued, "if Mr. Howard Hastings is a member here?"

"Indeed he is, sir. He is one of the founding members of the club."

I continued to press the point. "If *one* were to acquire the sponsorship of Mr. Hastings, might one be expected to be admitted as a member?"

"Certainly, sir. If one can obtain a recommendation from Mr. Hastings, he would have no trouble in gaining membership. Might one be interested in securing a recommendation from Mr.

Hastings?"

"One might," I said. By this time, I was tired of the snooty butler and decided to go back to the hotel and see if Howard would propose me for membership in his club. I knew he would. I hoped it wouldn't take too long for me to become a member.

I found Howard in the dining room having breakfast. After telling him of my adventure, he smiled and put down his fork.

"I don't know why I didn't think of that myself. Summerall and Carmichael are both members there," said Hastings. "I'll go there after breakfast and propose you for membership. All I need do is present your application with my signature and the signatures of two other club members and you officially become a member. I'll pay your dues when I'm there so there will be no delay in your application being accepted."

"Thanks, Howard. I really appreciate that. I would like to get in there just as soon as I can. Assuming you're able to get the application processed today, may I get you to join me there for breakfast tomorrow?"

"Indeed you may."

"That sounds fine. Let's meet in the hotel lobby at 7:00 am. We can take my buggy."

Hastings hurried off to the club while I went back to my suite. I needed to go through the rest of the documents I obtained at the library to see if I could find out anything more about the two men who tried to take over Great National.

***

Howard was waiting for me the next morning when I came downstairs. We got in the buggy and I took the reins and headed for the club.

I turned to Howard. "What do they call the club I've just joined?"

Howard laughed. "You may not believe this but we call it, The Club. It has a more pretentious name but I can't recall it now. Actually, your father was one of the founding members and he invited me to come join the next day. Most think of me as a founding member though technically I was not. Your father could be found here just about every day. Some days he would come at noon to share a meal with some of his colleagues. Other times he would come after work to talk with other businessmen before he went home. He believed a lot of business could be transacted there and he was right. On most days, one of us would be there at noon and the other in the late afternoon. It will be good to have you as a member."

"I never realized my father was a member," I said. "Certainly I'll be glad to follow in his footsteps in that regard, but today, my goal is to get closer to Summerall and Carmichael. How often do you see them there?"

"As I think about it, most of the time I've been there, I've seen them. And usually if one is there, they're both there. It makes me wonder if they ever do anything without the other."

We continued on to The Club. When we arrived, Howard

directed me around to the back where we parked the buggy. We entered through the back door and were immediately met by a doorman who took our coats and bowed deferentially. Howard led me from one room to another, pausing to speak with many men and introducing me to each of them.

As we passed one room, I saw Summerall and Carmichael. They had their backs to us so we passed without notice. In the adjoining room, Howard and I took a seat and were immediately brought plates of fruit. The room was paneled in dark walnut. The rug went from wall to wall and was deep red in color. The smell of tobacco filled the air though not many men were smoking this time of the morning.

As we took our last bite of fruit, a butler appeared and took our empty plates and replaced them with perfectly cooked eggs and sausage. But as I hungrily looked at the eggs, something caught my eye that took away my appetite.

At the door of our room, I could see Summerall and Carmichael walk out of their room and mount a sweeping staircase. I put down my plate and told Howard I was going to follow them. I kept my head down as I made my way to the stairs. They were about half of a flight in front of me. I watched as they reached the second floor and turned left. I arrived at the top of the stairs in time to see them disappear into a room toward the end of the hall.

They closed the door behind them so I feared I was out of luck in determining what they were talking about. As I walked down the hall I didn't meet anyone or hear any conversation from behind the closed doors. Near the end of the hall, I carefully opened the door adjoining the room Summerall and Carmichael entered. The lamp was off but I could see a bit of light near the corner of the room. As I explored, I realized it was coming from a butler's pantry that serviced both the room I was in as well as the one occupied by the two stockbrokers.

The door from the butler's pantry to the other room was a few inches ajar. As I approached the door I could hear the hushed voices in that room.

"Don't be so loud. I don't want anyone to overhear us," said the first voice.

"I'm not being loud. Besides there is no one upstairs except the two of us," replied the second voice.

"So what are we going to do about Hastings and Crudder?" asked the first voice. "If the fire didn't scare them away, I don't know what else we can do."

"Oh there's plenty more that we can do," came the reply. "We've only just begun to persuade them to sell to us. So far we've not failed to take every railroad we set our sights on. Great National will be no different. The only difference is it's larger than the others. It just makes sense that we will have to work harder to get it. But get it we will."

CHAPTER 20

As I listened, I could hear every word Summerall and Carmichael were saying. It was not clear which voice belonged to which man. What mattered most was the two men who had delivered such a blow to the American economy were in the next room plotting their next move.

"I don't see how we'll ever get Great National," said the first voice. "We have stretched ourselves to the limit to gather the stock we did when we thought we had half the company. Now we find out we own less than fifteen percent. How are we going to put together enough cash to buy a controlling interest? That's even if Crudder would agree to sell. And as of now, he's made it clear he's not selling."

The reply came immediately. "We just haven't been persuasive enough. Remember, even though Crudder grew up in the mansion, Hastings owned it now so maybe Crudder didn't have as much emotion invested in it anymore."

"Maybe so, but I hear that woman named Alvelda was badly burned. They don't know if she is going to live. And I heard that she practically raised Crudder."

"How did Mason and Evans get the entire mansion leveled?" asked the second voice. "I went by there this morning and it looks like the fire was so hot there is very little left other than a pile of ash and a chimney."

"Kerosene," said the first voice. "They poured gallons of kerosene all around the perimeter of the house and even poured some in each window that was open, and there were plenty of them open." Both men laughed as they reveled in the destruction their avarice had caused.

If I had any doubts as to who was responsible for harming Alvelda, they were all erased as I heard the two men laugh. And there was no doubt how these two would meet their end. As my anger boiled within me, I remembered the President had actually commissioned me to do what I was planning.

I continued listening and tried to remember all they were saying. The pain they had caused Alvelda was in the forefront of my mind. I think they talked about other railroads they were targeting but I'm not sure. What mattered most was they were not going to get to carry out any of their future plans.

Then the conversation took another turn and I listened closely to what they said because they were now targeting me.

"So the way we are going to get what we want is to take care of Hastings and maybe Crudder at the same time. With them out of the way, I think we can produce the documents we need to show Crudder sold us the company. And the funny thing is, it will not cost us another dime."

The two men laughed again. I could actually hear what sounded like them slapping each other on the back. My breathing became labored as my anger grew. Death would be too good for these two. I dared not even think of the horrible things I was contemplating.

"I wonder what a few sticks of dynamite would do to their office building?" said the first voice. "And wouldn't it be nice if it happened when Crudder and Hastings were both there?"

"How do you propose we get them both in the office at the same time?" asked the other man.

"I don't think we need to worry about that. We know Crudder is still in town. My guess is he and Howard will continue to be inseparable until Crudder goes back to Texas. And if we play our cards right, Crudder will not be going back home. He'll be joining his parents in the cemetery of Trinity Church."

Again the men laughed as though they had just heard a great joke. I was dumbfounded that men could be so evil to the core. As I continued listening to their plans, my anger began to subside. I guess it would be more accurate to say my anger went from hot to cold. Cold anger allowed me to think straighter and to not fear acting in haste.

"Where are Mason and Evans now?" asked the second voice. "They didn't leave town, did they?"

"No they didn't. In fact they are staying close to both Crudder and Hastings. They actually have rooms at the Fifth Avenue

Hotel."

"Are you crazy?" asked the second voice. "They can't be caught there. They might be connected to us and that would mean the end. All of our careful plans would be for naught."

"Listen, Buck. Don't treat me as a child. I know what I'm doing. No one saw either of them at the fire. And this is their first time in New York. There is no way anyone will connect us to them. And no one knows what they've been up to out-of-state."

"Sorry about that, Bill. I guess I got carried away. It's just this all seems too risky. What are you planning?"

"I think I'll get Mason and Evans to put their hands on as much dynamite as they can and make a visit to the Great National office Monday morning."

"You mean they just walk in and blow the place up?" asked Carmichael.

"More or less. Actually I've been in their offices several times. I know there's a closet near the lobby. If I'm right," said Summerall, "Hastings' office is on the other side of the wall. Mason and Evans can slip in there and plant the bomb. They can use a fuse long enough so they'll be able to get away before anyone sees them."

I had heard enough. In that brief conversation, I knew their next move. Silently, I slipped down the stairs and joined Hastings. He was still eating and my plate was on the table beside the chair where I was sitting. I had barely picked up my plate when Summerall and Carmichael descended the stairs. I averted my eyes and acted as though I was in conversation with

Hastings.

"...so the next thing I knew, I had lost track of the cattle. I rode back to the ranch house...."

"Well if it's not John Crudder and Howard Hastings," said Summerall as he pushed out his chest and hooked his thumbs in the pockets of his vest.

"It is indeed," I said. "And I see it's J. William Summerall and Buckminster Carmichael. I hope you're not here to try to sell me your stock in Great National. My offer was good only on the day I offered it. Now if you want to sell, I'll be glad to purchase your block of shares at the prevailing stock price."

"Mr. Crudder, we don't have any intention of selling," said Carmichael. "In fact, you may as well head back to Texas. We'll continue to buy shares of Great National when we get the chance. Just like we purchase other railroad stock as it becomes available."

"Funny you should say I should go back to Texas. That's what I'm planning to do just as soon as I can. I'll be glad to leave the business of New York with the three of you. Beginning tomorrow, Howard and I will be making some final plans for the future of the railroad. With any luck, I'll have our business wrapped up by the end of the week and can head back home."

"Well, safe travels to you, Mr. Crudder," said Summerall. "Good day, Mr. Hastings."

Donning their hats and putting on their topcoats, the two brokers left The Club. I quickly filled Hastings in on what I'd overheard.

"So Monday, we lie in wait for them at the office?" asked Hastings. "Won't that be dangerous for the employees?"

"What I have in mind," I said, "is for you to get in tomorrow and tell everyone they have the day off on Monday. Tell them it's a holiday bonus or whatever you like. I want to make sure no one is present when Mason and Evans come in."

"Then it will just be you and me confronting them?" asked Hastings. "John, I'll do what I can but you need to know I have never even shot a gun and I'm pretty much a coward when it comes to violence."

"Don't worry, Howard. I will be the only one in the office on Monday when Mason and Evans arrive. You stay at the hotel and be ready to send word to the President if something goes wrong and I don't return."

"John, don't talk like that. I can't bear the thought of something happening to you. After the death of your parents, it would be as though I was losing a brother."

"Snap out of it, Howard. Nothing is going to happen to me. I've been in tight places before. I don't intend to have any difficulty with those two. You just stay away and let me do what I need to do."

CHAPTER 21

When Monday morning came, I drove my rented buggy to the office. I tied the horse to the hitching post in front and wondered if anyone was watching me enter the building. If they were, they would be able to confirm I was dressed for a day in the office and I did look like I was there to take care of railroad business.

Others were coming to work next door and across the street but no employees were working at the Great National offices. I found an office just across the hall from the closet Summerall and Carmichael were talking about. It was a custodian's closet and it did indeed share a wall with Howard's office.

I left the lamp off and waited behind the mostly closed door. It allowed me a clear view of the lobby. I didn't have to wait long for the bombers to arrive. It was half past nine when the outside door opened and two men entered. One man was tall and slender and was wearing a six-gun on his hip. The other man was similarly armed but was much shorter—though still taller than me—and was carrying a large carpetbag. While I was not wearing a gun belt, I did remember to bring a gun. It had been in the pocket of my coat until the two men arrived. I retrieved it for I had the feeling things were not going to end well for the saboteurs.

The men entered quietly and closed the outer door behind them. They crept toward the custodian's closet and opened the door. As they did, I stepped out into the lobby.

"Don't either of you make a move," I said as both men instinctively raised their hands.

"Obviously you have been through this before. I didn't even ask you to raise your hands. But now that you have them there, make sure they stay up. You must be Mason and Evans."

The men looked at each other in surprise. It was clear they were the men I was expecting.

"I want to know how much Summerall and Carmichael are paying you? Whatever it is, it's not enough. The two of you are going to pay for what you've done. If you were in Texas, I think you would hang for your crimes."

As I spoke both men slowly let their hands move toward their guns.

"Don't try it. You'll never get a shot off. My aim is good. You'll be dead before you get your guns out of their holsters."

Against all odds, both men dropped their hands to their guns. I shot the shorter man first. My bullet struck him in the middle of the chest. As I shot, his gun went off with the bullet striking the floor. The taller man quickly got off a shot in my direction as I put a bullet in the middle of his forehead. Both men dropped to the floor and neither man moved. I kicked their guns away and opened the carpetbag. Inside was a stack of dynamite. It looked like there were forty or fifty sticks—enough I think to level the entire building. I was glad no one else was present just in case they had been successful in lighting the fuse.

I left the men where they dropped and exited the building. After locking the door, I got in the buggy and went down the street to the police station to report the attempted bombing. Immediately several policemen rushed outside and got in their own buggy. They shouted for me to follow. When we arrived at the building, I unlocked the door and stepped out of the way. It took them about fifteen minutes to completely investigate the scene. I think the presence of the bag full of dynamite answered any questions they had about whether the shooting was justified.

"Mr. Crudder, thank you for your cooperation," said the policeman who seemed to be in charge. "We're certainly glad you were here to stop them from blowing up your office. Judging from the amount of dynamite in the bag, I think they could've leveled this building and caused damage to the surrounding ones. You're free to carry on. We'll contact you if we need additional information."

A few minutes later they had the bodies loaded into a buggy and the policemen departed. *Two down and two to go!* I wasn't sure when I would get a chance at Summerall and Carmichael, but I was sure I would. Patience needed to be my watchword

Roy Clinton

CHAPTER 22

Back at the hotel, I went to Howard's room and told him what had transpired. His eyes were bigger than silver dollars as I told the story.

"…and then they drew their six-guns and fired. I had no trouble in ending their miserable lives. They didn't deserve a swift end for what they've done to Alvelda."

As much as I knew Howard agreed, he was in such shock he didn't respond. Not knowing the right thing to do for him, I changed the subject.

"Howard, I recall my father leaving a set of plans for the house in the desk in the office. I'm sorry we don't still have them so we could rebuild it as was."

Howard snapped out of his shock and his face lit up. "Funny you should say that. I'd been contemplating doing some remodeling. Nothing major and I was going to speak with you before I went forward with it. But several weeks ago, I took the plans to the office hoping to get an architect to look at them and tell me if what I was thinking was possible."

"I wonder if they're still there."

"I would imagine so," said Howard. "They're not actually stored in my office. I placed them in the top of the closet in the boardroom. I knew I would need a lot of space to spread them out. So even if Summerall and Carmichael changed things in the office, I'll bet they didn't have time to go through all the records."

"I would feel certain you're right about that," I said. "Howard, if you're in agreement, I'd like to have the mansion rebuilt just as it was originally—but with the changes you would like to make. It meant a great deal to me. It would be my pleasure to replace it at no expense to you."

"John, that's an amazing offer. I accept your generosity. Thank you so much. And as far as the changes I wanted to make, I think they might meet with your approval. As you recall, the basement and much of the first floor were designed to be servant's quarters. I don't need nearly as large of a house staff as there was when you deeded the mansion to me. As per your request, I retained all of them even though I had to look for things for some of them to do. Over the past few years, several have moved on and I didn't fill the vacancies."

"I wasn't aware of that, Howard. It doesn't surprise me you don't need as large of a staff. What did you have in mind?"

"Well, Alvelda had several times mentioned some changes that could be made to the kitchen to make it more efficient. She also mentioned some relatively minor changes to the second and third floors."

"I'm fine with whatever changes she wants to make. She's been here since shortly after the house was built. She has a better feel for what would improve the house than anyone else, including me."

"Well John, there's one more change I'd like to make."

"What's that?"

"Since we don't have the need for as many house staff, I'd like to turn part of the first floor into a suite for Alvelda. She's not nearly as young as she used to be. And after being injured in the fire, I don't know what she'll be able to do in the future. But even if she is able to return to her full duties, I was thinking about making her the house manager, but stress that this is a retirement job and I would expect her to spend the day doing just what she wants to do. And if she wants to do nothing, that's also fine with me."

Howard's heart for Alvelda caught me completely off guard. Tears began to puddle in my eyes. In spite of myself, I couldn't stop them. While I was sure he had seen her value in running the mansion, I wasn't sure he would have kept her employed had I not stipulated that when he started living there.

"Howard, I am completely on board with your plans. And I am very moved by your love for Alvelda. She's been very much a surrogate mother to me all my life. Even now with me not having regular contact with her, I often think I'd like to talk to her about things I am planning. And when you brought her to my wedding, I was touched too deeply for words to articulate."

I had been anticipating having Howard at the wedding since he was my best man. But I was stunned when Alvelda stepped out of the buggy behind Howard and held out her arms to me. Oh, how I prayed that she would survive. Alvelda understood me and accepted me and didn't ever make me feel I was in the way. She was never too busy for me. I find in the darkest moments of life, I sometimes escape by thinking of positive childhood memories of which Alvelda is always a part.

Anger burned within me. How could anyone hurt someone who had never brought harm on another person? While I knew Mason and Evans actually lit the fire that burned Alvelda, Summerall and Carmichael were ultimately responsible. Even if I had not been tasked by President Grant to find them and end the threat they posed to the United States, I was certain I would never be able to rest until they paid for what they did to Alvelda.

CHAPTER 23

The evidence I had gathered on Summerall and Carmichael showed clearly they were only interested in enriching themselves and they didn't care who they hurt. They left a trail of bodies and have financially ruined many people. So far they have been successful in keeping New York society of even suspecting them of any maleficence.

Howard and I were eating breakfast at The Club when we heard Summerall and Carmichael loudly greeting other members. Bill Summerall was the more boisterous of the two. He loved the spotlight and wanted people to know how important he was. In some ways it looked as though Carmichael was his acolyte. Summerall and Carmichael continued through The Club until they came to where Howard and I were sitting.

"And how are the railroad barons of New York City doing today?" asked Summerall, as he stuck out his hand to Howard.

Howard, ever the gentleman, rose from his seat, took

Summerall's outstretched hand and simply said, "Bill" in the way of a greeting.

I stood as Howard did and greeted Carmichael with a nod of my head and then took Summerall's hand when it was offered.

"I hope you fellows don't harbor any hard feelings about our desire to get into the railroad business in this city," said Summerall. "We already have modest railroad holdings in other states and thought it would be nice to have some interest in a railroad based in New York."

Modest holdings! That was an understatement. From what I had been able to ascertain, they had acquired enough smaller companies that, combined, now gave them one of the largest railroad networks in the country. We stood and listened as Summerall continued putting on a show for the rest of the members.

"And Mr. Crudder, I was pleased to hear that you were not hurt by the men who tried to destroy your offices," said Summerall.

Others in the room grew quieter as they listened to the news for the first time.

"You seem to be well informed, Mr. Summerall," I replied.

"Yes, I always try to stay abreast of happenings in our city. It was lucky you were able to stop the intruders. I hear you killed them both."

The room was silent waiting for me to respond but I said nothing.

"Well, Mr. Crudder, as I said, I'm glad you were not hurt in the episode."

Summerall and Carmichael stood motionless waiting for me to respond but I remained silent.

"Anyway," said Summerall, "we wish you gentlemen every success in your future ventures. And if you ever wish to sell, I think Buckminster and I would be interested in taking your little company off of your hands." He threw back his head and let out a laugh that could be heard throughout the room and then proceeded to shake hands with others who were in his path.

As Howard and I took our seats, I thought Summerall appeared more like he was running for office than coming to eat breakfast. I reflected on the spectacle I just witnessed. That's when I realized Summerall was indeed putting on a show to impress other members of The Club and perhaps garner some new business for his brokerage firm.

We resumed eating in silence when Howard turned to me and asked, "What was that all about?"

I leaned toward Howard and whispered, "He was either trying to direct suspicion for the bombing attempt away from himself or he was wanting me to know he was well informed as to the details of my daily life. They were interested in acting as though everything was normal and they were not connected to the plot in any way."

"Or," suggested Howard, "They could have been giving you a warning to be careful."

"I guess we'll find out," I said as I took a forkful of eggs.

After a few minutes, we saw Summerall and Carmichael make

their way upstairs. Howard turned toward me and arched an eyebrow. I pursed my lips and set down my plate. Nonchalantly, I started upstairs after the two were out of sight. It was hard to tell where they had gone. I knew there were only a limited number of choices.

I walked to the door of the same room where a few days earlier, I heard the malevolent men plotting the destruction of Great National's headquarters. There was no light coming from under the door so I quietly opened the door a few inches. The room was dark. Remembering the way to the butler's pantry, I walked with my hand touching the wall until I got to another door. Inside, I could see that the door to the adjoining room was once again slightly ajar. Getting as close to the opening as possible, I listened as the conversation got a bit heated.

"But I don't know anything about killing someone!" I knew it was Carmichael speaking and I could hear the panic in his voice.

"You have to do it," said Summerall. "There's no one else. Mason and Evans are gone. We dare not try to hire someone else to do the job. And we have to get Crudder out of the way if we're ever going to have a chance of taking over Great National."

"But I just can't do that. How would I even do it if I wanted to?"

"You get into his hotel room and shoot him."

"What?" cried Carmichael. "I could never do that! I'm not a brave man. I could never bring myself to kill someone."

"Sure you can," said Summerall. "You know we have already killed several people to get control of our other railroad interests."

"But this is different. We don't have someone else to do the work for us. I just wouldn't know how to go about it."

"It's simple. I have already found out where his room is located. He's on the sixth floor and his window overlooks the back alley. There's a fire escape ladder that leads to his window and even a platform outside his window to stand on." Summerall plunged ahead the way he always did and gave orders for how Carmichael was to proceed.

"Crudder probably keeps his window open a bit at night. All you have to do is to raise the window some, aim your gun, and shoot him."

Carmichael shook his head in disbelief. "And just shoot him! I can't do that. Besides someone will hear the shot and catch me."

"That's where you're wrong," continued Summerall. "You hold a pillow around the gun and it will muffle the sound."

"If it's so easy, why don't you do it?"

"Carmichael, you can't expect me to do it. I'm an old man. I couldn't even get up the ladder without huffing and puffing. And I'm not nearly as strong as you. You, on the other hand, will not have any problem getting up the ladder quickly and taking care of Crudder. Then you just quietly climb down and walk away. I'll even be in the next block with a buggy to take you home. Simple."

"It may be simple but it's not as easy as you make it out. I can see many things that can go wrong. And if I get caught, I'm the one who will go to Auburn Prison. You won't have to worry about a thing."

"Buck," said Summerall, "we've done well up to this point. But for us to realize our dream of having a monopoly on the railroad industry in this country, we have to have Great National. Crudder is the key. Unless he's eliminated, our dream is over."

Summerall was silent for several seconds. He seemed to sense Carmichael was weakening. I listened closely but heard nothing. Had they stopped talking because they realized someone was overhearing them? My heart began racing. Had I made noise as I got closer to the opening into their room?

I turned to leave to keep from getting caught. As I turned, I heard Carmichael respond in a low voice. "All right. I guess I can do it. I don't like the idea at all but I'll do it if there's no other way. When do you think it should happen?"

Summerall responded, "I think it needs to be done tonight. We need to make a move before any more time passes. Crudder is a danger to our plans. The longer he is here, the more likely he is to try to find a way to stop us. You go tonight. I'll pick you up just after midnight. We'll drive to the hotel and I'll wait for you while you take care of Crudder. It will all be over in a few minutes. You just wait and see. It will be the easiest thing you've ever done."

The silence from Carmichael let me know he was not convinced. It also told me I wouldn't get much sleep that night. The door of their room opened to the hallway and as it did, someone turned down the lamp. I waited in darkness until I was sure they left the building.

Downstairs, Summerall and Carmichael found Howard by himself just finishing his breakfast. They approached him and Summerall asked, "Where's Mr. Crudder?"

"Well, he—uh—had some business to take care of. He should be back soon."

"Well, speaking of business, Buckminster and I need to get back to our offices. Good day, Mr. Hastings."

"Good day, Mr. Summerall. Mr. Carmichael."

I could hear their conversation plainly from my vantage point at the top of the stairs. When they left The Club, I rejoined Howard.

"It looks like tonight is going to be an exciting time at the hotel," I said to Howard. Howard was speechless and utterly shocked as I told him of the late night visitor I was anticipating.

"John, you need to go to the police," said Hastings. "You can't take a chance on getting killed."

"Don't worry, Howard. I'm not going to get killed. You should know by now I can take care of myself. Besides, the President asked me to take care of this problem personally. Actually, he asked Midnight Marauder to take care of it."

"How can you be so calm?" exclaimed Howard. "I know I will not get a bit of sleep tonight! And my room is nowhere near yours!"

"Calm down, Howard. You don't have to worry about me. By the time we're having breakfast tomorrow morning, there will be one less conspirator for us to worry about."

Roy Clinton

CHAPTER 24

Howard went to the office to try to get some work done. I doubt he was able to concentrate on anything other than to fear what was going to happen in my room that evening.

My day was rather busy. First, I went to a luggage store a few blocks from the hotel and purchased a steamer trunk and had it delivered to my room. Then I thought it was a good day to take a buggy ride. I left the luggage store and headed north. I got on Riverside Drive that runs parallel to the Hudson River, and let my horse adopt an easy trot for several miles.

After about thirty minutes, I found what I had been looking for. There was an abandoned warehouse with a pier extending into the river. I surveyed the area and didn't see another person. A side of the warehouse was open and there was a four-wheel dolly sitting by the door. The whole area was deserted.

Returning to my hotel, I went to my room, saw that my steamer trunk had been delivered, undressed, and took a leisurely nap. As it turned out, I slept straight through until after eight o'clock. The room was dark when I woke up.

I dressed but put on casual clothes. My activities for the rest of the evening didn't require office attire. Downstairs, I went to the dining room and found Howard was midway through his meal.

"Good evening, Howard."

"Oh my goodness! You startled me!" Howard's hands were shaking so much that food fell from his fork.

"Howard, what's gotten into you? You're as nervous as anyone I've ever seen."

"John—I—well—you should be nervous, too." He leaned closer to me and whispered. "How can you be so relaxed knowing someone is getting ready to try to kill you?"

I smiled, not because it was a foolish question but because of Howard's true concern for me.

"Because it is just as you said. Someone's going to *try*. I plan on making it my business to see he'll not succeed. Thanks for your concern for me. Just try to relax. This will all be over before long."

The waitress arrived and I placed my order. When she left, Howard leaned over to me and whispered, "Just be careful. I don't want anything happening to you."

"I appreciate that, Howard. But you can rest assured that nothing is going to happen to me." He nodded in agreement though his eyes belied the gesture.

By the time my food arrived, Howard had settled down somewhat. He was not as visibly nervous but he clearly had lost his appetite. When I finished my meal I told Howard I would meet him at The Club for breakfast at our usual time and excused myself.

Returning to my room, I arranged pillows on the bed and covered them with a blanket to approximate the look of someone sleeping. Then I opened the window closest to the fire escape ladder, turned down the lamp, and waited in the darkness. It would be several hours before Carmichael arrived. I pulled a chair over to the other window so I could see down into the alley. There was enough light that I thought I would have no trouble seeing Carmichael before he could get into my room.

About half past midnight, I heard a buggy at the end of the alley. Someone climbed down and the buggy continued on out of sight. The man walked quietly up the alley toward the hotel. While I couldn't make out the person's identity, I was sure it was Carmichael. That was confirmed when the figure walked up to the ladder, looked all around, and then climbed the ladder to the landing outside my window.

Reflecting on Summerall's idea as to how to restrict the sound of a gunshot, I picked up a pillow from the sofa and wrapped it around my gun. As I walked over to the fire escape platform, I saw the window open further and an arm extend through the opening.

I aimed carefully and shot Carmichael once as he was taking aim at the bed where he supposed I was sleeping. Summerall was right. The shot sounded only as a muffled *pop*. I grabbed Carmichael by the lapels and pulled him into the room.

The steamer trunk was already open so I slid Carmichael's body inside. Interestingly, there were only a few drops of blood. He must have died instantly. I cleaned the floor as well as I could and added the towel I used—as well as the pillow that silenced my gun—to the trunk and secured it with the padlock I purchased from the luggage store.

I went downstairs and asked that my buggy be hitched and for a bellman to bring a dolly to my room. When the bellman arrived, I asked him to take the trunk downstairs. He took it to my buggy and I helped him load it. He made no comment about the weight of the trunk or the request to load it after midnight. I guess he must have had similar requests through the years. The five-dollar tip I gave him disappeared into his pocket and he quickly turned and went back into the hotel.

The air was crisp and cool though not as cold as it usually is this time of year. I guided the buggy over to Broadway since it had streetlights. After about twenty minutes, I turned and went over to Riverside Drive. I could see the abandoned warehouse coming into view. It stood sentinel overlooking the Hudson River. Carefully, I looked around to make sure no one was watching. I drove the buggy into the open side of the warehouse and slid the trunk down onto a dolly I spotted earlier in the day.

There was a large stack of bricks against one wall that I used to completely fill the remaining space in the trunk. I wheeled the trunk through the warehouse and out onto the pier. Near the end of the pier, I pushed the trunk, dolly and all, into the Hudson. There was a significant splash as the trunk hit the water. I waited for a minute to see if anyone heard the disturbance. The only sound I heard was from the steam whistle of a ship that was about a mile down the river.

Silently I bowed my head and removed my hat. *Well, Lord, I guess Carmichael got what was coming to him. All it seems he was interested in was getting richer and he didn't care who had to die to make that possible. I commend him to your keeping.*

I returned to my hotel hoping to get a few hours of sleep before breakfast. As I lay down, I couldn't help but go back in my memory to the town council in Bandera and how each of their lives had ended. I had hoped to put that type of business behind me and I think I would have had the President not pressed me into service. There was still one more person to deal with.

Roy Clinton

CHAPTER 25

Howard was once again nervous as I joined him for breakfast at The Club. He wasted no time in asking questions about the previous evening.

"How did it go?" whispered Howard.

"Just as planned. No problems. No complications."

"Did you bury him?"

"In a manner of speaking."

"What's that supposed to mean?" Howard's whisper was elevated and came out as more of a hiss.

"He's at the bottom of the river."

Howard looked at the floor as his shoulders shuddered. This ordeal had shaken him to the core. It was one thing for him to know what I had done in Bandera but quite another to know what happened in the hotel just a few doors down from his room.

As we talked, Summerall entered The Club. He looked around the room as was his practice but this time he didn't stop and chat with many other members. This day, he was noticeably subdued.

He stopped and spoke to a few men. There was a noticeable absence of his sidekick. One of the members even asked about Carmichael. Summerall claimed not to know and said he had probably gone into his office early. Then he headed over to our table.

"Morning, Mr. Crudder. Mr. Hastings."

This time I kept my seat and continued eating. "Hello Mr. Summerall," I said. "How may we help you this fine morning?"

"Oh, there's nothing you can do. I'm just passing through on my way to meet some friends for breakfast. By the way, I guess there is something you could do for me. Did you see Mr. Carmichael last evening? He said he was going to drop off some papers at your hotel."

"Mr. Carmichael never gave me any papers," I said and then turned to Hastings. "Did he give you any papers, Howard?"

Howard choked on his sausage and began coughing and couldn't stop. The offending piece of sausage shot from his mouth and bounced off Summerall's trousers while he continued to cough. Summerall looked at the stain on his pants and let out an audible groan.

"I'm sorry, Mr. Summerall," said Howard between coughs. "I'll be glad to pay your cleaning bill."

"That's not necessary, Mr. Hastings. Did Mr. Carmichael come see you last evening?"

"No," replied Howard. "I haven't seen him since the two of you were here yesterday morning."

"Very well," said Summerall. "If either of you see him, please tell him I was looking for him."

"We certainly will," I said. "Mr. Summerall, I just hope you have not misplaced him. Maybe he decided to take a trip," I suggested.

"That's foolish talk. Where would he go?" asked Summerall.

"Maybe he decided to take a cruise on the Hudson," I replied.

Howard had a look of alarm on his face as Summerall huffed and turned away.

"Good bye, Mr. Summerall. I have a feeling you will be joining Mr. Carmichael very soon."

As Summerall left the room, Howard turned to me, visibly shaken. I stuck a fork in my sausage and raised it to my mouth as I said, "Got to look out for these little things, Howard. You never know when one will slip up and take your breath away.

Howard put his hands to his face and then put his elbows on his knees. I knew I would need to get Howard out of there for he looked as if he might faint. We got up from the table and went out to our buggy.

"John, what were you thinking? It's like you were purposely agitating Mr. Summerall."

"I'm sorry, Howard. I didn't mean to make you uncomfortable. But you're right, I was purposely agitating Summerall. He and his compadre have much to atone for. It's not just the many people they've killed as they put together their railroad empire or even the fact they tried to take over Great National. When they harmed Alvelda, it became personal to me."

Roy Clinton

CHAPTER 26

We left The Club and went by the hospital to check on Alvelda. When we got to her room, we were pleasantly surprised to find she was awake and was even able to smile at us.

"Johnny boy. Just look at you."

I walked to Alvelda's bed and wanted to hug her but she appeared to be bandaged all over. A nurse who was tending her rose and stopped me.

"She is much improved but you can only stay for a few minutes. The doctor asked me to come get him if you came by. I'll be back in a few minutes."

Reaching down to Alvelda, I looked for a place where I could touch her but little of her skin was not bandaged.

"Oh Alvelda, I'm so sorry you got burned." Tears fell from my eyes unexpectedly.

"Don't cry, Johnny boy. Ol' Alvelda's gonna be all right. You know something like this can't keep me down."

"I'm so glad you're getting better. I don't know what I'd do without you."

"Johnny boy, you're not gonna find out 'cause I'm still here and plan on being here for a long time."

Dr. Maxwell and Dr. Gross entered the room and began checking on Alvelda.

"Our patient looks like she's turned the corner," said Dr. Gross. "One of the things in our favor was her burns were confined to her face, arms and legs. Her clothing kept her from being injured worse. I'm glad Dr. Maxwell got me here when he did. He was able to start her burn treatments immediately, and I was able to modify those treatments with my latest adaptations, which significantly improved her survival chances.

"One of the problems we face when we're dealing with massive burns is the loss of bodily fluids. We have been able to manage that well and now just need to give Miss Alvelda time to heal. And heal she will. Eventually she will need some skin grafts but we'll tackle that later."

Dr. Maxwell added, "Dr. Gross, it was John Crudder here that insisted I contact you. He insisted Miss Alvelda have the best burn treatment available."

"Mr. Crudder, I'm glad you had Dr. Maxwell contact me. We were able to save Miss Alvelda and it was good to get to work with Dr. Maxwell again."

"Gentlemen, you have my deepest thanks for what you have done for Alvelda," I said. "I had planned on telling you this later but before I leave New York, I'll be making substantial contributions to your institutions. Dr. Gross, I have already contacted Jefferson Medical College and understand their greatest need is for a new medical amphitheater to teach young surgeons. I am providing the funding for that. It is my understanding they will call it the Gross Clinic.

"Dr. Maxwell, it seems Bellevue Hospital has many needs. The gift I am making to the hospital will provide a new building that will take care of several of those needs. However, I am stipulating that you be the one to direct specifically how funds are used."

Neither doctor spoke for several seconds. Then Dr. Maxwell said, "If I truly get to direct the use of the funds then I am going to see the name of John Crudder emblazoned on the new building."

"I appreciate your thoughts, Dr. Maxwell. But I would appreciate it if my name was not associated with it at all. What you can do is find something smaller in the hospital that you can name in honor of Alvelda."

"We can certainly do that," said Dr. Maxwell. "I have an idea. I know we need a new dining facility. We could name that in her honor."

"Doctor," said Alvelda.

Her voice stopped the impromptu meeting that was taking place in her room. I immediately felt bad that I brought up any business while she was convalescing nearby.

We turned back to Alvelda to see what she needed.

"Not the dining room," said Alvelda.

"I'm sorry, ma'am," said Dr. Maxwell. "I'm not following you."

"Not the dining room. The kitchen. Call it Alvelda's Kitchen."

We all exchanged a smile. Through her bandages, it looked like Alvelda was smiling with us.

"Alvelda's Kitchen," said Dr. Maxwell. "I like it. I'll make sure that happens."

Howard and I walked out of Alvelda's room and were joined by the doctors in the hall.

"Are you sure she is going to be all right?" I asked Dr. Gross.

"Yes, she is on the mend. She does have a lot of healing yet to do but I am no longer concerned as to whether she will survive. She is getting the best care we can give and it has made a difference."

"I'm relieved to hear that," I said. "My business is almost completed here. I'll be returning to Texas before the week is out." I looked at Howard. "In fact, Howard, if you can get me a train ticket for Kansas City to leave the day after tomorrow, I think I can get my business wrapped up."

"I certainly will, John," said Howard.

CHAPTER 27

Howard and I took the buggy from the hospital to the Great National office. It was good to see the office filled with workers and know that the company had withstood the takeover attempt. We went into Howard's office and shut the door.

"So what's next, John?"

"I've checked out Summerall's house. He appears to live alone. I think I'll visit him tonight."

Howard's eyes darted side to side and his hands started to shake.

"Calm down, Howard. Don't worry about a thing. I hear Summerall's health is not good. I wouldn't be surprised if he simply died in his sleep."

"John, I don't know what you have in store but be careful."

"You don't have to worry about me. I'll be fine. Now just arrange a ticket for me on the train to Kansas City. It's time I get back to Bandera. There're just too many people in New York to suit me."

I left the office and took the buggy out by Summerall's house. It was situated on a street that had few houses. His house was the only one in his block. I left the buggy and walked around to the back. No one was around so I jimmied the lock and let myself in. On the second floor I found several bedrooms but quickly realized only one was being used. In that room, the bed was unmade, and clothes were on the floor. Summerall wasn't much of a housekeeper and it appeared he didn't have any regular hired help.

I let myself out and took the buggy back to the hotel. The rest of the day was spent finalizing plans to leave town. I completed the arrangements for the contributions to Jefferson Medical College and Bellevue Hospital.

As I contemplated my return to Bandera, I realized I had been so caught up in railroad business I had not done any Christmas shopping. I was determined to get home for Christmas and I didn't want to go empty handed.

I took the buggy to Lord and Taylor on Broadway and Twentieth Street. The store had everything I could imagine under one roof. It didn't take me long to find two new dresses and hats for Charlotte. I also bought her two pairs of shoes and a new handbag.

The sales lady who was helping me led me to the children's section and helped me select dresses for Claire and Cora. I also got each of them a doll. There was one last purchase to make. I wanted Slim to have a pocket watch. There were several to choose from. The one I selected was made by Waltham and had a solid gold case.

I returned to the hotel and packed up the gifts. There wasn't much left for me to do except wait until evening when I had an appointment with Summerall. At suppertime I went to the dining room and placed my order. I was surprised not to see Howard as he was usually there when I arrived. When my meal was served, I waited a few minutes hoping Howard would join me. Finally, I decided he was probably not coming so I went ahead and ate.

Just as I was finishing, Howard joined me.

"John, I'm so glad you're still here." Howard looked more flustered than he had over the past several days. "I just came from the office. I had a meeting with Summerall."

"Summerall? Why on earth were you meeting with him?"

"I didn't plan it. He came in just as I was getting ready to leave. In fact, my secretary had already left so he just barged into my office. John, I don't have to tell you I was very concerned when I saw him. I thought he might be there to harm me."

"What did he want?"

"At first, he acted like he was just there for a friendly visit."

"We both know that was not what he was after."

"Yes," said Howard. "I knew there was more to it than that but at least that's the way it started out."

"So what did he really want?"

"He said he had it on good authority that we were trying to take over his railroad holding and force him out of business." Howard rubbed his hands together and continued in an agitated tone. "He said he knew that is the reason you came to New York and he wasn't going to let that happen. He even accused me of trying to turn Carmichael against him. I told him I didn't know what he was talking about. I've never even seen Carmichael alone. And I've only seen the two of them together at the first board meeting that they tried to take over and then at The Club a few times. John, he was talking crazy."

"Howard, try to calm down. What else did he say?"

"Well, he said he knew President Grant had been in town a few weeks ago and he knew that we met with him. John, I don't know how he found out about that. I certainly didn't tell anyone."

"Don't worry about it. It was not a secret the President was in town. From what he said, he and his wife get here often to take in the theater. And it doesn't matter if he knows we met with him."

"That's not all." Howard opened his eyes as wide as possible and started rubbing his hands together again. "He said that Carmichael was missing and he thought I was responsible. John, I didn't know what to say. He could tell I was nervous. And when he mentioned Carmichael, I know I must have seemed even more nervous. John, he thinks I did something to Carmichael! What will I ever do?"

"Get a hold of yourself, Howard. This is not a time to panic. Summerall doesn't have any evidence concerning Carmichael. He was just there trying to scare you...."

Howard interrupted and raised his voice. "Well he did a good job of it!"

"Shh. Howard, lower your voice. He was just trying to

intimidate you and hope you would give him some information. What happened after he accused you of causing Carmichael to disappear?"

"He said if Carmichael doesn't show up at The Club in the morning, he's going to take his suspicions to the police. He said he would own Great National before he was through. And he said you and I would both regret the day we were born. John, what am I going to do?"

I reached across the table and put my hand on Howard's arm and squeezed.

"Howard, you have to calm down. Nothing is going to happen to you. Summerall is not going to harm you and he's certainly not going to take over Great National. In fact, in just a few hours, Summerall will breathe his last." Howard mumbled to himself and continued rubbing his hands together. "Relax and know all of this will be behind us by morning."

I left Howard at the table and returned to my room. There was nothing more I could do for him. He was inclined to be a bit of a worrier anyway. That is one of the things that make him so valuable to the company. He stays on top of the many things that need to be attended to and seems to be able to juggle multiple jobs at a time.

Back in my room, I had time to kill. I pulled out a book I had started reading on the train. It was a new book by one of my favorite authors, Jules Verne. It was titled *Around the World in Eighty Days*. It is the fascinating story of a man who accepted a wager that he could travel around the world in eighty days. I can really get lost in a good book. Before I realized it, the evening had nearly passed.

A little before midnight, I picked up a candle and placed it in my pocket. I then put on my coat and hat, went downstairs, and found my buggy at the curb in front of the hotel, just as I had instructed the bellman. I tipped him generously.

"Thank you, Mr. Crudder," said the bellman. "Out for another evening ride?"

"Yes, I like the night air. Though it's quite a bit colder than it was the other evening. I will probably not be out late. When I come back, would you mind taking care of my horse and buggy?"

"It would be my pleasure, Mr. Crudder."

I popped the reins and headed out for Summerall's house. When I arrived, I stopped the buggy where I had earlier in the day and carefully looked for light in each of the windows. I walked around to the back of the house and again listened for any indication that there was anyone stirring inside.

The back door was easy to get opened. Inside, I listened and could hear the rhythmic breathing of Summerall. The house was completely dark. As much as I didn't want to, I had to light the candle so I could find the staircase. Carefully, I climbed the stairs and then turned toward Summerall's room. He was still breathing slowly and heavily.

I crept into his room with the candle still burning. There was a risk the light would awaken him but it was too dark without it for me to see. When I got to his bed, I set the candle on the bedside table. I reached up my right sleeve and withdrew the dagger than I had previously only used in Texas.

With my left hand, I put the dagger to the edge of Summerall's ear canal and clamped my right hand over his mouth. He awakened with a start as I slid the tip of the blade further into his ear.

Summerall's eyes were fully opened and his hands were grabbing for me.

"If you're smart, you'll quit struggling. That sensation you feel in your ear is my knife. Struggling will only make your pain greater. You know who I am?"

Summerall nodded that he recognized me.

"I'm going to release your mouth. But I must warn you. If you make any sound other than to answer my questions, your end will come prematurely."

I released my grip on his mouth but kept the dagger in place.

"John, what on earth do you think you're doing? You have no right to be in my house. And what are you doing with that knife?"

"I'm here to serve justice on behalf of the United States of America and at the direction of the President."

"Justice for what?"

"You and Carmichael have badly damaged the economy of our country and you did it all out of greed. If you're not stopped, we know you will continue to destroy the railroad industry and who knows what else."

"Listen John, you're a businessman. Surely you can

understand that the things I did were just business. I've never caused anybody any harm."

"That's where you're wrong, Summerall. You and Carmichael have had many innocent people killed and many more financially ruined just so you could enrich yourselves."

"John, that was just business."

"Quit saying that, Summerall. It was not *just business* when you had your men rig the boilers on several locomotives to explode. And it was not *just business* when you had the warehouse burned down. Many have lost their lives simply because you were pursuing your *business.*

"And it wasn't *just business* when you burned down Howard Hastings' mansion and nearly killed one of the people who is most special to me. Summerall, your time is up. Tonight, you go on to meet your Maker."

With those words I plunged the dagger deep into his brain. His body stiffened but then relaxed. I withdrew my knife and placed my finger over the ear canal. Using my other hand I took some of the warm wax from the candle and rolled it into a ball and then molded it to the opening of his ear. I straightened the sheets and blanket and centered Summerall's head on the pillow.

Removing my hat I bowed my head. *It's me again, Lord. William Summerall was well thought of by many in this city. But few knew of the evil that marked his life. You know all about that and I know You will determine where he spends eternity.*

There was no evidence I had been in the room other than a bit of wax on the table. I removed it, walked back downstairs, got in my buggy, and drove back to my hotel.

That night I slept well, knowing I had accomplished my mission. I did what the President had asked me to do. At the same time, I made sure Great National was still in good hands with Howard at the helm. And I had avenged Alvelda's injuries.

Roy Clinton

CHAPTER 28

My last day in New York was a day of tying up loose ends. I visited with Alvelda. We reminisced about my childhood and of the many things we did together. She told story after story about me and with many of them she laughed as she relived the details. It was good to see her laugh. Even though the doctors told me she was out of danger, it was her laugh that finally relieved my anxiety about her health.

The train for Kansas City was scheduled to leave at three in the afternoon. I went by the Great National office to see Howard and pick up my ticket. His secretary greeted me and told me Howard was expecting me. When I entered his office, he was sitting at his desk taking care of business.

"John! Come in and have a seat." He walked over and closed the outer door. "Did everything work out last night?"

"It did indeed. I would predict that later today, Mr. Summerall will be discovered to have had a heart attack in his sleep and never woke up."

Howard got that nervous look on his face again and started to rub his hands together.

"As I said, Howard, everything worked out fine. There is nothing to worry about. And the best part for you is there will not be anyone else trying to take over Great National."

Howard sank heavily onto the sofa. "I'm glad this whole business is over." Then he lowered his voice to a whisper. "And I'm glad we don't have to hear any more about the Midnight Marauder. If it's all the same to you, I wish he would just ride off into the sunset and stay there. No offence meant to you, John."

I laughed. "I share that sentiment, Howard. I don't anticipate him being needed again. But you have to admit there's a certain comfort that comes from knowing he's only a telegram away."

"You're right about that. Thank you for all you've done. And thank you for your foresight in retaining controlling interest in Great National. I'm so glad the company will continue and not be broken into pieces as Summerall and Carmichael intended."

"I appreciate the compliment. But as I said a few days ago, my reluctance to sell Great National had more to do with me not being sure what was the wisest decision. What I've learned is I will never again entertain the thought of selling what you and my father built. I know you are one of the most significant reasons for its success."

Howard's eyes slowly left mine and looked toward the floor. Tears formed great pools in his eyes and spilled over onto the rug. "Thank you, John. I appreciate you saying that. I'm just pleased to have had the chance to work alongside your father for so many years."

"While we are on the subject," I paused and gathered my thoughts, "I would like for you to attempt to purchase all of the outstanding stock in Great National. Offer a premium if you need to. I want this railroad to once again be a privately held company."

"I'll do that. In fact, I've found out a large block of stock is available and was going to ask you about purchasing it."

"I'm glad to hear that, Howard. And contact Carmichael's company and make an offer to buy his interest in Great National. Later this week, you can do the same with Summerall's company."

Howard nodded his head in agreement and went to his desk to make notes of our conversation.

"Well, I guess I need to be making my way to Grand Central Depot. Does your secretary have my ticket?"

"There's not a ticket, John."

"Oh?" It was not like Howard to miss important details. He knew I wanted to get home by Christmas. Leaving today was cutting it closer than I wanted but if I missed today's train, it was likely I wouldn't get to enjoy Christmas with my family.

He chuckled as he saw my concern. "Don't look so worried, John." There was a twinkle in his eye. I could tell he was enjoying watching me get worried for a change. "You're going to get home on time. You will be on the train to Kansas City. I took the liberty of having your father's private coach attached to the end of the train. Actually, it's two cars. One is for you and the other contains a kitchen and sleeping quarters for the staff."

"Private coach? I never knew my father had a private coach."

"He had it built a few years before his death. He realized the best way for him to keep up with what was going on in the company was to get out of the office and personally check on the company interests in other states. It was a good decision for it allowed him to continue work as he would when he was in the office but also allow him to get out and check on other parts of the company. I've even used it a few times and find it to be very useful."

That made sense to me. I was just surprised I had never heard of the existence of the private rail car. "Thank you for arranging that. It will be an interesting ride, that is for certain."

I stood and said, "It's time for me to get to the depot. Thank you, Howard, for all you've done for me and for my family."

"It is I that should thank you, John. I appreciate you taking a chance on me by retaining me after your parents died. I'm not sure what life would have looked like if you had not done that."

"You're welcome. I know you're a man of integrity and I know of your loyalty to the company and to me. Frankly, that was the best business decision I ever made." As we shook hands, Howard continued to cling to mine. Finally he released it.

"So long, John. I'll keep you up-to-date on Alvelda's recovery."

"Yes, please do. So long, Howard."

I left the office intending to go straight to my train. Then I remembered that I needed to send a couple of telegrams. Stopping at Western Union, I scribbled out two messages and handed them to the attendant. I had to search my memory for the name of the President's assistant. Then I remembered.

Jeffrey Jameson
Washington, D.C.

Mission accomplished. S and C are no longer a problem. Permanent solution found. Glad to be of service. Please address any response to me in Bandera, Texas.

John Crudder
New York City

The second telegram was one I have wanted to send since I arrived in New York City.

Charlotte Crudder
Bandera, Texas

Headed home. Expect me by Christmas. Love,

John Crudder
New York City

When I arrived at Grand Central Depot, I had a porter take my trunk and suitcase to the end of the train. One thing I had not considered was how I was going to get my luggage back to Bandera. I had several suits and multiple shirts I picked up in Fort Worth. I also had the gifts I bought for the family.

I followed the porter to the end of the train. There I was greeted by three uniformed staff.

"Good afternoon, Mr. Crudder. My name is Giles. I am your butler. I am in charge of the staff and in personally attending to your every need."

"Hello Mr. Giles." I extended my hand but Giles politely bowed instead of extending his. "You may just call me John."

"I'm sorry sir, but I will never be able to call you John. I know my station in life and I am comfortable with it. And sir, it is not Mr. Giles. Just Giles." He bowed again but this time he put one hand at the waist and the other to his back. As he bowed, I found myself beginning to bow in response but stopped myself before I dipped too deeply.

"Sir, this is Simmons. He is your personal chef."

The chef bowed deeply as well. This time I was able to remain still and simply nodded my head a bit and said, "Simmons."

"And this is Rosser. She is your chambermaid. She is also responsible for keeping your coach spick and span. She will also clear and clean your dishes after each meal."

I touched my hat and said, "Rosser."

"Now sir, if you will follow me, I will show you to your coach." As we entered the car, Giles pointed out each feature. I was struck with the richness of the walnut paneling. Every bit of wood was beautifully stained and buffed to a satin finish. The rug was deep maroon in color and extended throughout the car. On one side of the coach was a leather couch that was flanked by side tables, each of which featured lamps with shades in multiple colors. On the other side of the coach was a table with drop leaves that would accommodate at least six. Down from the dining table was a desk that was set with writing paper, an ink well, pens, and a lamp.

At the far end of the coach was a fireplace that already had a fire burning. Nearest the platform end of the car there was a grouping of chairs with side tables. Windows lined three walls making the car bright and sunny. Each window was fitted with a shade that matched the rug. Beyond the fireplace was a small hall that led to the bedroom and a private commode and bathtub.

Giles stepped back and motioned for Simmons to enter the car. "Simmons will tell you about dinner and answer any questions you have about meals.

"Mr. Crudder," Simmons began, "for this evening, I am preparing steak, cooked medium rare as Mr. Hastings said you like it. I am also serving lobster, baked potato, green beans, and a salad. In the cabinet beside the fireplace you will find a full bar with an assortment of libations. May I inquire as to what you would like for breakfast?"

"A couple of scrambled eggs with a single piece of sausage would be nice. And a bit of fruit if you have it."

"We do indeed have a variety of fruit, sir. Is there any particular kind you would prefer?"

"No. Just a bit of whichever fruit you have handy." I didn't really know how to say what was on my mind without hurting the feelings of the staff but I plunged ahead anyway. I turned toward Giles but then rotated eye contact to each person. "I appreciate all of the trouble you've gone to in order to make me comfortable. Dinner sounds like it will be most enjoyable. I look forward to it. This will be only the third time I've tried lobster so it will be a special treat. But after today, I would prefer simple meals—the same food that you are eating.

"And as far as my needs on this journey, I'll not require much. At water stops, it would be nice to have a newspaper if one can be found. I will not need anything from the bar. In the evening, it would be nice to have a glass of beer if it's available. Water is fine if you don't have beer. Beyond that, I'm sure I'll be fine. I'm not used to having anyone wait on me. I hope I don't seem ungrateful. I'm just a simple rancher from Texas visiting a friend in New York who thought it would be a nice thing to send me home in this luxury train car."

"Very well, sir," said Giles as he bowed. On cue Simmons bowed and Rosser curtseyed. "No one will ever enter the car without invitation. There is a button on the table by the door and another in your bedchamber. They are connected to a buzzer in the next car. If you require assistance, I will come immediately after you push the button. If I wish to enter or when your meals are ready, I will activate a button in our car that will ring the bell that is on the wall beside the fireplace."

"May I get you anything now, sir?"

"No thank you, Giles. I'm fine." The three again showed deference and exited the coach down the hall beside the fireplace. I assumed they were headed to the next car that contained their living quarters.

I had a seat near the platform and looked out the windows as the train left the depot. When it got up to speed, I went out to the rear platform, stood and watched the last of the city disappear into distance.

I was duly impressed by my surroundings. Knowing my father, I had no doubt this train car was the finest private coach in the country. While I would enjoy my ride to Kansas City, I couldn't wait to get home to my family.

Roy Clinton

CHAPTER 29

After four days in my luxury surroundings, I arrived in Kansas City. I boarded the stagecoach for San Antonio and spent nearly two weeks eating dust and wishing I were back on the train. In San Antonio, I found a buggy for sale, loaded it with my trunk and suitcase and Midnight's saddle. I tied Midnight to the back of the wagon and headed to Bandera. Travel by buggy was much slower than it would have been if I had been riding Midnight. A little over halfway to San Antonio, I made camp and ate a can of cold beans and a can of peaches. Even though I had not been riding Midnight, I knew he would appreciate a good brushing. After I finished grooming him, I brushed the buggy horse, and climbed into the back of the buggy on a pallet I had made for the evening. As I lay there, Christmas carols were playing in my memory. I hummed several as I fell asleep.

At first light, I was hitched up and was soon ready to travel. It was Christmas Eve and I was eager to be home. This time, I didn't tie Midnight but let him run alongside the buggy. I knew he wouldn't get far from me. When I arrived in Bandera, I went by the telegraph office and found I had a message from the President's assistant.

John Crudder
Bandera, Texas

Thank you for the assistance provided by you and your friend. I hope you will not mind if I call on you again.

Jeffrey Jameson
Washington, D.C.

I wasn't sure what the President meant when he indicated he might call on me again. But if the need does arise, I'm glad to be of service to my country. Leaving the telegraph office, I turned the buggy toward the H&F Ranch. Midnight loped ahead knowing we were going home.

EPILOGUE

Daddy come home?" asked Cora.

"Will he?" echoed Claire.

"His telegram said he would be here by Christmas," replied Charlotte. "You know he will do everything he can to be with us just as soon as possible."

"I just hope the stage didn't encounter any delays," said Slim. As had been his practice, he spent the evening with Charlotte and the twins.

"Daddy!" shouted Cora. Both girls ran to the front door and greeted me as I rode up. I put on my best singing voice, trying to bring them a bit of Christmas cheer.

Deck the halls with boughs of holly, Fa la la la la la la la la!
'Tis the season to be jolly, Fa la la la la la la la la!
Don we now our gay apparel, Fa la la la la la la la la!
Troll the ancient Yuletide carol, Fa la la la la la la la la!

Charlotte and Slim clapped and Cora and Claire squealed as they met the buggy. I climbed down and caught one daughter in each arm and hugged them tightly as they showered my cheeks with kisses. I put the girls down, turned to Charlotte, and held out my arms. She ran into them and I enveloped her with the embrace I had anticipated giving her since I left New York.

Slim came over and slapped me on the back. "Welcome home, John. I'm so glad you made it for Christmas."

We walked into the house with Cora hugging one leg and Claire on the other. I couldn't help but laugh as I thought about how full my life was. I knew I was a blessed man. The house was beautifully decorated for Christmas. A large wreath was on the front door and there were flowers and greenery throughout the house. A Christmas tree stood in the corner of the living room. It was draped in tinsel and ribbons. There were strings of popcorn encircling it and presents underneath.

"I didn't know you could sing," said Charlotte. "Sing some more."

"Daddy, sing," said Cora agreeing with Charlotte. I lifted her into my lap. As I did, Claire held out her hands indicating she wanted some lap time too. With both of my girls in place and Charlotte and Slim sitting by the fire, I sang another carol.

The First Noel, the Angels did say
Was to certain poor shepherds in fields as they lay
In fields where they lay keeping their sheep
On a cold winter's night that was so deep

Noel, Noel, Noel, Noel
Born is the King of Israel!

Once again, my family clapped. My heart was full as I reflected on how happy I was to be there with them.

"I have some presents in the buggy if anyone is interested."

"Yeah!" said the twins in unison.

"Slim, if you'll help me bring the trunk in, the presents are inside."

I opened the trunk and gave the girls their dresses and dolls. Charlotte was properly surprised by her dresses and hats. She remarked that the handbag was perfect.

Charlotte went to the tree and brought back a box for me. I unwrapped it and inside found a soft leather wallet. "I saw that at the mercantile and thought it looked handsome."

"It is lovely. Thank you, sweetheart. Thank you, Cora and Claire." Both girls returned to my lap.

"And there's one more present." I reached into the trunk and found a small box and held it up for Slim to see. "I would bring this to you but my arms are full at the moment."

Slim retrieved the box and opened it. He was speechless as he looked at the beautiful gold watch.

"John, I don't know what to say. This is a fine watch. I never thought I would own one like it."

"I'm glad you like it, Slim. I figured with you being mayor now, you needed to look the part. That watch will help you look more mayor-like, though I don't know if it will make you a better mayor."

"Thank you, John. You have become the son I have never had."

"All right," said Charlotte. "Enough of that sentimental stuff. You men stop that or you'll get me crying. John, how about one more Christmas carol?"

"Just one more," I said. "Then I know two girls that need to get to bed." I thought for a moment and as my daughters shifted in my lap and turned their faces toward me, I began to sing.

I heard the bells on Christmas day,
Their old familiar carols play,
And wild and sweet the words repeat,
Of peace on earth, good will to men.

Slim went to his house and Charlotte and I tucked the twins into bed. As we prepared to sleep, I told her about becoming a special agent to the President of the United States, about the fire that burned Alvelda, and the outcome of my work over the past four months. She listened spellbound to the stories I told. I was glad to be home and for the adventure to be over. It was good to hold Charlotte in my arms again.

Later that night as I was falling asleep beside my wife, I wondered what was in store for me next. The New Year was just a few days away. I knew life in Bandera had been one adventure after another. Whatever was ahead, I was sure what I wanted above all else was peace on earth and good will to men.

ACKNOWLEDGMENTS

I would like to say thanks to my wife Kathie, who was the first to read this book and give helpful edits; to Sharon Smith, whose work makes me appear more literate; to beta readers Teresa and Phil Lauer, Richard Barnes, Philip Placzek, Chris Bryan, Michael Porter, and Max Morelli. Your suggestions helped make this novel better. If you would like to be a beta reader, get manuscripts before anyone else, and have a chance to shape the final book, please email me at Roy@TopWesterns.com.

As with my other books, I have sought to be historically accurate in as many details as possible. The Panic of 1873 was indeed a crisis that impacted the whole world. In fact, until the depression in the twentieth century, it was called the Great Depression. The information about Jay Cooke & Company is factual however Summerall and Carmichael were characters created only for this book.

There really was a Dr. Samuel Gross of Philadelphia. The

burn treatment described was developed by him and was responsible for saving the lives of many burn victims. Dr. Thomas Maxwell, the Chief of Medicine at Bellevue Hospital, is fictitious. I would like to thank my oldest grandson, for allowing me to use his name for this character. Who knows, perhaps someday there will be a Dr. Maxwell Thomas Morelli.

President U. S. Grant was indeed a heavy cigar smoker who ultimately died of throat cancer. History has not been kind to Grant, ranking his administration as one of the worst. However, he had a deep impact on the country both because of his presidency and also because of his role in the Civil War.

The mass hanging in Bandera is fact and is presented in this book as close to what actually happened as could be determined. Visitors to the city can see the hanging tree and read about that dark period in Bandera's history. Also idioms, phrases, and figures of speech used in this book are all period correct.

I'm always glad to hear from readers. You may email me at Roy@TopWesterns.com. I make it a point to answer every letter. Please be patient if it takes me a few days to respond. I may be on a writing retreat or traveling but I will reply.

The next book in the *Midnight Marauder* series will be released soon. The title is *Love Child.* You may read a preview on the next few pages

NATIONAL BESTSELLING AUTHOR

ROY CLINTON

LOVE CHILD

A MIDNIGHT MARAUDER ADVENTURE

Roy Clinton

LOVE CHILD:
A MIDNIGHT MARAUDER ADVENTURE

Roy Clinton

PREFACE

February of 1874
BANDERA, TEXAS

Mayor, I don't care if you don't think it's your business. We elected you mayor and we expect you to do something about it!" The part of Slim Hanson's responsibility as mayor he liked the least, was listening to complaints from citizens who felt he was obligated to look into every concern or problem anyone in the town faced.

"Mrs. Mercer, I can understand you and Mrs. Grimes not getting along. But she must live about a mile from your place."

"Actually, it's closer to two miles. But when she comes to town, she takes the wagon road that is right in front of my house. Every time she passes, she sticks her nose in the air and says

"Humpf."

"She says what?"

"Humpf. And I want you to do something about it."

"But Mrs. Mercer, there's not anything against the law about that." *How did I get myself roped into this? Trying to reason with her is like trying to reason with that old heifer on the H&F that keeps getting stuck when she sticks her head between the rails of the fence.*

Slim continued trying to reason with the disgruntled woman. It did no good to tell her that was not his job or that her neighbor wasn't breaking the law. He figured there was something deeper going on, and as much as he wanted to help, he knew he just didn't have the patience needed to find a solution.

"Mrs. Murphy, you and Mrs. Grimes used to be the best of friends. At least that's how it looked. Any time one of you was in town, I knew I would see the other. You never went anywhere without each other. What happened to that friendship?"

"I'll tell you what happened. Last month at the church social, *she* baked a pie using my recipe. And *she* took credit for it!"

"Let me get this straight," said Slim. "Mrs. Grimes baked a pie and took credit for baking the pie?"

"No. She took credit for the recipe."

"Just how did she do that?" Slim could feel his patience coming to an end.

"It was *my* apple pie recipe she used. Her pies never did come out right. But she used my recipe and when people complimented her on how good the pie was, she just said 'thank you' and let

246

them go on believing it was her recipe."

"Did she actually tell anyone it was her recipe?"

Just then, a teenage boy came walking in the office behind Mrs. Mercer.

"I'll be with you in a minute, son," said Slim as he tried to direct his attention back to the crisis of the moment.

"What did you call me?" asked the boy.

"I didn't call you anything, son. I just said I'd be with you in a minute."

"There, you did it again. Why do you keep calling me son?"

"I'm sorry. I meant no harm. I should have said, 'young man, I'll be with you in a few minutes.'"

Slim thought, *every time I come to town and go to the mayor's office, I face the same thing. People bring their problems to me. And as I try to help, it seems I always offend someone.*

"Now what were you saying, Mayor?"

Slim tried to remember what the conversation with Mrs. Mercer was even about. "Did Mrs. Grimes actually tell anyone it was her recipe?"

Mrs. Mercer thought about it for a moment. "No, Mayor, I don't remember her doing that. But she just let people think it was her recipe."

"Mrs. Mercer, maybe Mrs. Grimes just didn't know how to take the compliments she received."

Slim got up from his desk and lowered his voice as he moved closer to Mrs. Mercer.

"Besides everyone in town knows Mrs. Grimes is not that

great of a cook and they also know you make the best pie in town. With you bein' neighbors and all, I doubt anyone seriously thought her pie makin' suddenly got that much better. I'll bet everyone at the social was secretly remarkin' at how nice it was for you to lend Mrs. Grimes your recipe."

Mrs. Mercer's face brightened. "Do you really think so?"

"I know so. It's no secret you're might near the best cook in all of Bandera. And you certainly make the best pies anyone's ever tasted. I'd imagine, people all over town are still talkin' about how nice it was for you to help your neighbor, so she wouldn't be embarrassed at another social."

"I never thought about it like that, Mayor. You know, I think you're right. Now that I think of it, I saw several of the women smiling at me when Mrs. Grimes was being complimented. Thank you, Mayor. I knew you would have a solution. I'm glad we elected you. Well, I have to go now. Please give my best to Charlotte."

"I will Mrs. Mercer. Thanks for comin' by."

As she was walking out, Marshal Williams walked into the office and went immediately to the stove and poured him a cup of coffee.

"Mornin' Slim," said the marshal.

"Howdy, Marshal.

"What's Mrs. Mercer got a bee in her bonnet about?"

"It seems there was some confusion over who gets the credit for the recipe Mrs. Grimes used last week when she made a pie for the church social," said Slim.

"Thought she was all tuckered out about that by now" said the marshal. "She's been to my office twice this week talkin' about the same thing. I'm just glad you were in town today so she would come talk to you and give me a rest."

"I hope we've heard the end of it. By the way, Clem, did you see that boy that was in my office? He must have left just before you walked in."

"Yup. But don't know his name. He's been hangin' 'round here for the last couple of weeks. I've seen him sweepin' up over at the Cheer Up a couple of times. Last week, he was over muckin' out stalls at the livery. Seems like he's always workin'."

"Any idea where he came from?" Slim asked. "There's somethin' familiar about him but I just can't place it."

"No. He just showed up here one day. Next thing I knew he was workin' for different merchants. He don't seem to be causin' no trouble. Did he cause any trouble here?"

"Oh, it's nothin' like that Clem. He just seemed a might touchy. I was just wonderin' who he was."

Slim and the marshal finished their coffee and walked out of the office when Slim spotted the boy across the street at the Cheer Up. He had a broom in his hand as he walked into the saloon. Slim was sure he must have met the boy before but he couldn't place his name. The boy was about fifteen or sixteen and had very dark brown hair but his eyes were between blue and brown. He had a dark complexion and was already nearly six feet tall. Slim thought he was going to be a big man when he was fully grown.

Slim's curiosity got the best of him so he walked over to the Cheer Up and looked over the swinging doors. There were a few cowboys standing at the bar and a few others were sitting down playing cards. Slim spotted the boy in the back of the saloon. He walked over to the boy and called out to him.

"Pardon me, son. You came by my office earlier but didn't wait around. What was it you needed?"

"Why do you keep calling me that? Why do you call me 'son'?"

"I meant no harm. If you tell me your name, I can address you more properly."

"My name is Richie."

Slim stuck out his hand and said, "Pleased to meet you, Richie. You can call me Slim."

Richie shook Slim's hand. "I can't do that. It wouldn't be respectful. I'll just call you mayor."

"That's fine Richie. I like a boy with good manners. Have we met before? I could swear I've seen you before but I don't remember where."

"No. I'm sure we haven't met before."

"Why don't we sit down a talk a bit, son—I mean Richie." The boy propped his broom against the wall and took a seat across the table from Slim.

"Do you live 'round here Richie?"

"I guess I do now. I'm really from Laredo. But I've been here about a month."

"What are you doin' in Bandera, Richie? You're a long way

from Laredo."

"My mother always told me if something ever happened to her, I was to go to Bandera."

"Did she tell you why she wanted you to do that?" asked Slim.

"No, she just said things would be better for me here if something happened to her. She even said I had some family around here."

I need your HELP!!

Willing to write a review on Amazon?

Here's how :
1) go to amazon.com
2) search for Roy Clinton
3) click on appropriate title
4) write a review

The review you write will help get the word out to others who may benefit.

– Thanks for your help,
Roy Clinton

Made in the USA
Middletown, DE
09 November 2020